RABBLE ON A HILL

Shad Holly and Nat Towne are brought together when they are involved with a British patrol in the streets of Boston. Shad, an experienced frontier fighter, and Nat, a young actor, eventually are engaged in dangerous missions during the siege of Boston. Both are among the defenders of Breed's Hill, a name not so well known as nearby Bunker's Hill, thanks to the confusion of British army cartographers.

RABBLE ON A HILL

BY ROBERT EDMOND ALTER

ILLUSTRATED BY ALBERT ORBAAN

WILDSIDE PRESS

To Larry Sternig

CONTENTS

Military power will never
awe a sensible American to
tamely surrender his liberty.

Samuel Adams, 1768

PROLOGUE

The men who boarded the *Dartmouth* and the *Eleanor* and the *Beaver* looked no more like Mohawk Indians than a clown looks like a prime minister. But it didn't matter because there weren't enough British troops quartered in Boston at the time to do anything about it, and the disguise was only a token disguise—a handful of feathers and some warpaint and even an actual tomahawk or two.

So, with a thousand or more spectators standing mutely on Griffin's Wharf, about a hundred of the "Mohawks" (who wouldn't fool a four-year-old imaginative child) dumped and destroyed 342 chests of tea, valued at £18,-000, because they didn't want any American to have to pay the tax on it—let alone drink it if he didn't feel like it.

That was in the close of 1773, but the news didn't reach England and the King until March of '74, and when he heard the good tidings he nearly had a fit. What were those fool Americans thinking of? He was the King of England, wasn't he? And America was an English colony, wasn't it? And if he said that his subjects were going to drink the tea and pay a tax on it besides, then by George, that's what they were going to do! Whether they liked tea or not.

He also said (after he'd calmed down a mite): "The line of conduct seems now chalked out . . . the New England Governments are in a state of rebellion. Blows must decide whether they are subject to this country or independent."

Then he decided to slap the naughty Americans on the

7

wrist to teach them a little lesson so that they would know how to behave themselves the next time some loudmouth like Sam Adams or John Hancock or Dr. Warren came up with a harebrained scheme. He appointed General Gage governor of the province of Massachusetts (with 4,000 regulars to back him up), and on June 1 the Port Act went into effect.

Boston Harbor was sealed off from the world by a tight blockade. No ship could enter, no ship could leave. Everything came to a standstill. Trade rolled over with a groan and died. Merchants closed their shops and tore their wigs. Idle, jobless men roamed the streets and loafed on the docks. And without the lifeline of the sea, Boston was a hungry town.

And an angry one.

The yeast of discontent was beginning to ferment into violence. Secret organizations such as the Committee of Communications, the Committee of Safety, the Sons of Liberty, and the Minutemen sprang up overnight, and all along the eastern coast men began to gather weapons and powder and lead for ammunition, and they formed militia companies and drilled in the commons and in the fields and in the roads.

Farmers and merchants and sailors, dock workers and clerks and backwoodsmen, lawyers and doctors and rowdies were preparing for war.

I

H-HERE'S YOURS

Somewhere on Orange Street a crystal crash went *pow!* in the night, as though a glass grenade had exploded. Instantly there was hooting and cat-calling, and a brawling voice rose above the tumult.

"Run, Tory, run!"

Nat Towne turned into the first shadow-locked alley. He wasn't about to get himself involved with a Boston mob. These brawls occurred every day, every night now, all over the city. One moment a street would look like any street minding its own business; the next moment some hapless fellow would come somersaulting through a doorway or—if no door was handy—crashing through a lead-paned window, with three or four men raging after him, and he would take off down the street, his unfriendly companions pelting after him; and then, and seemingly from nowhere, other men would spring up, and all at once everyone would be shouting ear-covering language, and the sticks and bricks and fists would start to fly, until the crimson smear of red-coats with their bright dazzle of bayonets would appear and put the mob to rout.

9

"No thank you," Nat said. He would just as soon keep his head uncracked, if it was all the same to everyone concerned. Why Benny Frazer had ever thought it advisable to move his troupe of thespians into this hotbed of anger was more than Nat could understand.

He supposed the fool still clung to the futile hope of being able to straddle the fence, wearing a two-way coat showing a loyal lapel on one side and a rebel lapel on the other. And maybe he was right: maybe Boston was the last town in America where a man could at least attempt to walk the middle of the road.

Nat stayed with the alleys, coming into the open only when he had to cross one of the main streets. Behind him the tumult was increasing like an advancing sea, which meant that the mob was having a real knockdown and dragout tonight.

He was halfway across the lantern-bathed cobbles of Tremont Street when three rowdy-looking individuals came rushing past him strung in a line like geese on the wing. The last man was a scrawny fellow with a stick in his hand, and he paused to glare at Nat belligerently.

"Which side are you, brother?" he demanded.

It was one of those questions to which the answer was too often like "heads I lose, tails you win." Nat made fists of his hands and leaned slightly forward from the waist.

"That's my business, brother."

The scrawny one hesitated, sizing the youth up. Nat was only eighteen, but there was six feet of him and his shoulders were impressively broad.

One of the other men looked back and yelled: "Come on, Jerry! Afore the giddy patrol picks us up!"

It was a good enough excuse for the scrawny man. He

wagged his stick at Nat and took off, calling back: "Get you later—Tory!"

Nat watched the three rowdies diminish down the gloom of the street, their driving legs chopping at the greasy-looking cobblestones. Then, as a sudden shrill *ta-weee* of a whistle blew nearby, he got himself off the street, darting into the nearest black mouth of an alleyway.

It was a short passage, and you could see the two-sided opening at the far end like a candle behind an oilpaper window—and the moment he plunged into it he realized he had picked the wrong alley.

Two silhouettes, as sharply defined as though they had been clipped out of black tin, were in a death-grip struggle in the center of the alley. The one, the taller, stumbled on something underfoot and lost his balance and toppled backwards against the brick wall, as the other, shorter, silhouette sprang after him.

Something flashed in the man's back-swinging hand, paused for a split-second, long enough for the blade to catch a thin red light from one of the distant streetlamps and for the light to dance along the edge like blood. Then he swung it underhand and forward, and Nat heard the heavy, shocked grunt that jerked from the man against the wall.

The shorter man stepped aside as he watched the other man tilt slowly and stiffly away from the wall and topple past him. Then he looked up, and he couldn't help but see Nat's silhouette looming toward him.

He went into a crouch, and again the blade caught a glint of light and winked, as he sprang over the prostrate man and came at Nat in one quick hunched bound, hissing: "H-had to h-have a look, didn't you? Well, h-here's yours!"

Nat leaped backward, snatching the tricornered felt hat

from his head and swung it down and into the passage of the glinting, underswinging knife, and the blade came paring cleanly through the crown and was deflected off course, flashing right on up and almost into Nat's armpit.

Off balance and not certain of his target (the assailant had veered to the left and out of the frame of lamplight), Nat swung with his left and felt his fist collide with wool-covered flesh and knew his aim was off by a foot. He had connected with the man's shoulder. But it was a good blow and it was enough. It got the man and the knife away from him.

He crouched in the dark, sucked in his breath and held it, listening, waiting for the man to give his position away.

Ta-weee! The whistle blew again.

Nat heard a sudden rush of movement swish by him and saw the running silhouette of his enemy appear briefly in the wan light of the Tremont Street entrance. Then he was gone, and Nat was alone in the alley with the prostrate man.

He was on his way out. The sound known as the death rattle was already in his throat as Nat knelt over him.

"Po-powder horn," the man gasped.

"What?"

"Take the—the powder horn. Don—don't let anybody get it. Promise."

What he was talking about Nat had no idea. But it was obvious that the man was dying, and so he said: "All right. I promise."

He felt the man's body in the dark. His clothes had the tactile quality of deerskin. On the man's left hip Nat found a powder horn.

"Mister, who did this to you? Who was the man with the stutter?"

"To-tor———"

"Tory? Was he a Tory?"

But the man had nothing more to say.

Nat stood up with the horn in his hand. Slowly, reflectively—a little awed by the near proximity of death, actually—he wound the rawhide thong around the horn and shoved it into his jacket pocket. There was nothing more he could do there in the alley. It was time to go.

The whistle went *ta-weee* on Tremont Street, and Nat started to run toward the opposite exit—right smack into a huge, black, up-springing apparition that seemed to loom over and around him like the stern of a Concord coach. He grunted *"Uuh!"* as they collided and rebounded: but not far. The monster caught his right arm in a viselike grip, and Nat opened his mouth to yell—too late.

A hamsized hand slapped around his mouth, and Nat watched a burly head topped with a cocked hat lean down to him and saw two small porcine eyes peering at him with dangerous intensity.

"Brother," the big man whispered like the rasp of a file, "all I want from you is *one* word. Are you Tory or are you a patriot? Now when I remove my hand, don't you go to yell. Because even though my mitt is somewhat big I'll ram it inside your mouth and pluck out your tongue like I was takin' feathers offn a fry chicken."

Nat was ready to believe the big man could do it. He felt the hand step off his face, and he treated himself to a fresh breath of air.

"Well, I'm an American," he said warily.

The big man nodded his head and gave Nat a pat on the shoulder that felt uncomfortably like a near dislocation.

"That suits me. Listen, I'm Shad Holly and I'm from

Pennsylvany and I'm in a *lee*-tle bit of trouble with them lobsterbacks."

"You mean you were in the riot tonight, and now the regulars are after you."

"Did I say that, brother?" Shad Holly demanded angrily. "Do I look riotous to you? No, I weren't in no riot. I was just takin' my evening stroll down Orange Street when a batch a rily fellas went to belaborin' each other with sticks and stones and I don't know whatall, and me just standin' there watchin' the show, when all at once this here fat-mouth lobsterback captain comes chargin' around the corner and starts callin' me all sorts of blue names."

Shad Holly blew out his breath gustily.

"Now I don't mind being called a rebel or even a Boston mobster, but when he went to call me *fat*—well, he went one word too far."

In spite of his anxiety, Nat found himself fascinated by Shad Holly's bombastic manner. "What did you do?" he asked.

"*Do!* What did I do? Well, what would you've done? I couldn't have that fool standin' there talkin' that way with mebbe some ladyfolks hearing him from their windows. So I reached out my hand to close his mouth—sort a like I just done to you. But I was so excited I got confused, see? And I somehow forgot to *open* my hand. Anyhow, he lost two, mebbe three front teeth because of my mistake.

"Say, you ever see a lobsterback captain that's lost a few buck teeth? My goodness, how he carried on! He didn't even wait to pick hisself up off the street afore he's yellin' and slobberin' and spittin' all over hisself for his men to put holes in me. I tell you, the only thing that saved me from lookin' like a porkypine growing baynets was that his men couldn't quite get the hang of his slobbery words right off, him not used to havin' no front teeth to bank his tongue offn.

"I was going to tell him that there warn't no sense in him kickin' up such a fuss over just a few buck teeth, 'cause I know this fella Washington, and he has some real dandy whalebone teeth and can talk just as good as you or me. But no, this here lobsterback won't let me get a word in for all the watery noise he's making. So I lit out."

Which was what the two of them had better do right about then, Nat figured. "Come with me," he said. "I've a place you can hide till morning."

But just then Shad Holly discovered the dead man.

"S-a-y, I don't want to appear nosy, boy, but you mind tellin' me just who it is we're standing on top of?"

"Another fella put a knife in him. I'll tell you about it later. Let's get out of here."

"Brother," Shad said hoarsely, "the next time I don't know I'm standin' over a dead man for ten minutes yammerin' my big mouth, you just hit me over the head with something handy will you? C'mon, let's make fast tracks!"

2

"WHAT NEWS?" CRIED ROBIN

The last alley brought them to the stage entrance of Benny Frazer's theater. The door safely closed behind them, Shad blew out his breath and said: "I don't know as how I think too highly of actors, by and large, but I'd certainly rather be here than in Boston's Stone Jail!"

In the lanternlight Nat was able to examine the complete Shad Holly, and there seemed to be no end of him to examine. First off, he was probably the biggest man in America (Nat thought so, anyhow). He was six-four at least, not counting his boots and hat, and he had to weigh over 260. He was maybe fortyish, and his face was perfectly round and sunset pink and aglow with sweat. His eyes were small, angry, curious, lively eyes, and all in all he looked like a mighty rampant man.

He removed his hat, which anyone could see at a glance had once belonged to a British officer, and wiped at his brow with a great bandana that looked like a soiled French battle flag.

"That's a fine hat," Nat said. "How'd you come by it?"

Shad seemed a trifle vague about the acquisition of the

hat. As best as he could remember he'd stopped at a tavern in Providence on his trip north and there had been a batch of British officers in there raising the old Nick, and when they somehow or other got the impression that Shad was a Loyalist, they filled him up with free ale, and when he left the tavern he went to the table where he'd parked his coonskin cap among all the officers' hats and—his wits being a mite befuddled—he must have picked up the wrong hat by mistake.

"I often wonder what that major looks like in his dress uniform with my coonskin cap on his head," Shad mused, brushing at the silver lacework on the cocked hat.

He was, he told Nat, in the Pennsylvania militia, and the Committee of Communications had sent him up to Boston in February with some vital information for the Boston Committee of Safety.

"How is it you're still here?" Nat wondered. "I thought they sent you fellas back and forth."

"Why, any fool knows trouble is comin' atween the British and the Americans. And most of us knows that when it does come it'll be started by these here Yankees. And, boy, I aim to be right here handy when it happens!"

Old Elijah Simp, the gnarled, bent-nearly-double property man, came hurriedly by them with his peculiar crabwise shuffle, shaking his head.

"Best look spry, Nat," he warned. "Old Benny's throwing a fit backstage on account you're late and Ralston hasn't showed up yet."

That was bad. Nat and Ralston were supposed to present a new act that night: the Robin Hood and Little John jousting scene. It had already been advertised; and now no Ralston. But it was no great surprise to Nat. Ralston

Morbes was an avowed Loyalist, a Tory. He was probably embroiled in some mischief or other out in the streets.

"Come on, Shad. I'll tuck you away in one of the dressing rooms."

But they never made it. With a mighty "Ah-ha!" Benny Frazer descended upon them, his gravy-spotted velveteen waistcoat flapping about his narrow concave torso, a curl of his wig loose from its pins bobbing up and down by his right ear. He wigwagged his pipestem arms at Nat melodramatically.

"So. So. We've decided to make our appearance, have we? We've elected out of the goodness of our heart to give our fellow performers the benefit of our estimable presence! So good of us! So generous we are! And where is our boon companion Master Morbes, pray tell?"

Shad blinked at the scarecrow of a man, and turned to Nat.

"Say, just how many of *you* is he talkin' about?"

"I don't know where Ral is, Benny," Nat said. "There's trouble in the streets tonight. My friend Mister Holly and I ran into some of it."

Benny snatched his floppy wig from his bald head and threw it *spamp* against the back wall. Not satisfied with that, he took a running jump at it and landed on the powdery old moth nest with both feet.

"Gads and all the goldfish of Greeves!" he wailed. "Ruin! Utter, undeserved, unappeasable ruin! And a full house out front for once! And no Robin Hood. They'll tear the stage down! I know they will. I've seen it happen before. I———"
His voice slammed to a halt and he studied Shad like a beady-eyed bird of prey.

"The *size* of him! Mark you the size of him! The *perfect*

Little John!" Benny came hop-hopping over to grab Nat. "Nathaniel—man that I've raised from childhood—we will switch parts, sweet lad! *You* will play Robin, and this monster—that is to say, this *gentleman* will play Little John!"

Shad's eyes were beginning to glimmer and glower. "Now hold on here. What is all this Robin and Little Johnny talk, anyhow?"

Benny went after the enormous Shad with fluttery, eager fingers.

"Why, you've heard of Robin Hood the famous bandit of Sherwood Forest, surely! Nat here was supposed to play Little John to Ralston's Robin Hood. Ah-ha! But now we will give him Robin's part and *you* will be our Little John!"

Shad's face clamped down like a public house closing for the night.

"Now look here, toothpick! I don't usually mind folks referrin' to my size, but there's one thing I ain't, and that's *little*!"

"But you don't understand, dear sir," Benny hastened to assure him. "Little John is a name meant in jest. Little John was in truth an enormous man. His name was but a joke——"

"And that's something else I ain't is a joke," Shad said dangerously. "Now I don't mind helpin' you fellas out, 'cause Nat here helped me tonight. I'll be this Rob-bandit Hood fella, if you want. But I ain't about to go around pretending I'm some dwarf called Johnny! And that's flat!"

Benny snatched at his head for his wig but found only baldness.

"Benny," Nat said, "if he's willing to give us a hand, let's· not argue about it. Besides, I've already learned Little John's part."

"The part! The part!" Benny looked around in a state of wild distraction. "He must learn the part, and not a moment to spare! The curtain rises! The manuscript! Who in the name of all the foul fiends has pilfered the manuscript? Who——"

Old Elijah nudged his elbow and calmly handed him a few dog-eared sheafs of paper. Benny snatched them up and turned back to Shad.

"Now then, good Master Holly. Listen attentively! The lines are few and simple. Should your memory suffer a lapse, a hesitation, a dislocation, simply cry 'What news?' "

"What news?" Shad echoed blankly.

"Yes. Robin was forever crying 'What news' to everyone he encountered in the forest. Don't ask me why. Now then; Nat's on stage when the curtain ascends and he says: 'Here I am Little John the brave! I am the mumble-mumble and so on . . . and I shall cross me over this instant.' " Benny pointed at Shad. "That's your cue."

"My who?"

"Cue! Cue! You enter now." Benny ducked his nose back into the script, reading: " 'What news?' cried Robin. 'Whence comes this gangling creature I see towering over me? Speak your name, varlet!' "

Benny pointed at Nat, still reading: " 'Little John is my name, little man,' spake Little John. 'And I desire to cross yon log——' "

"Hold on here," Shad cut in. "Is that *spake* kin to a spade or a stake? How does a fella go about spakin' hisself?"

Benny crumpled the script in despair. "It means spoke! *SPOKE!*"

"Just wanted to know, brother," Shad said mildly. "That's all."

The balky curtain rose slowly before Nat, showing him the glare of the footlights in their tin reflectors. Beyond the blaze of tallow candles the small sea of expectant faces was but an indistinguishable glimmer of dark flesh with here and there the spark of an eye. He wet his lips apprehensively. He was very dubious about the outcome of the scene. And, to make matters worse, the audience had had to wait twenty minutes while Shad learned his lines, had his grease paint applied, and was helped into costume; now they were turning unruly.

They scoffed rudely at the sight of Nat standing before them in tight green-cloth pants and jerkin and a silly little scotch cap surmounted with a turkey feather. He grounded the butt of his seven-foot "yew" staff and leaned slightly toward the hooting audience.

"Here I am Little John the brave! I am the tallest, broadest, strongest yeoman in all of merry old England! I——"

"Which makes you a dad-gasted Tory!" a disembodied voice yelled from the audience, and a rotten tomato near-missed by Nat's ear with a hum and went *splamp!* on the painted backdrop behind him. The audience roared with appreciative laughter.

Yes—he was *very* dubious about the outcome.

"I see before me a stream with but a single log for a footbridge, and I shall cross me over this instant." Nat turned to the "stream," an old dead log about seven feet long chocked on a pair of blocks concealed behind wooden "bushes." On the upstage side of the log (where the audience couldn't see it) was a huge, shallow tin pan of water. Literary legend and Benny's script had it that Little John was supposed to knock Robin off the log and into the water. Which suited Nat. He'd had his bath last Saturday.

Now, having spoken Shad's cue, he hesitated. No Shad, or Robin.

"I shall cross me over this instant!" he repeated, hopefully.

The audience started to hoot again. "Do you need some help, Tory?" "Which instant was you talkin' about, Johnny? Next week's?"

All at once a monstrous parody of Robin Hood was literally propelled upon the stage from the wings by Benny, old Elijah, and three or four other grinning thespians.

Shad Holly, his sausage-tight cloth suit perceptibly bursting on his massive body (half the buttons having already popped off), his face whitened with grease paint and a thick up-curled paper mustache glued to his upper lip, the feather in his cap gone awry and bobbing down in front of his face, lurched toward his end of the log and promptly dropped his staff on his toes.

Nat figured the people over in Charlestown could hear the roar that issued from the audience. "Hi, Little John! Did you say you was the *tallest* or the *smallest!*" "Say, ain't you two merry men kind of twisted around?" "Why don't you fellas hang signs to yourselves so we'll know which's Robin and which's Little-*tiny* John!"

One look at Shad's stricken face assured Nat that his huge friend's mind was a complete blank. Shad had been struck dumb by that well-known thespian ailment, stage fright. He looked so utterly gargantuan in his ridiculous costume and with that strained expression of baffled bewilderment on his great moony face that the audience continued to greet him with volley upon volley of raucous laughter.

"I shall cross me over this instant?" Nat repeated helpfully.

Shad picked up his staff, sucked in his breath, and cut loose.

"What news, cried Robin!" he bellowed.

"No no!" Nat hissed. "Not *Cried Robin*: just *What news.*"

"What news!" cried Shad. "Fence comes this spaking creature I see towering over me?"

The audience went wild again. Nat "towered over" Shad about the way a toadstool towers over a grizzly bear. And then it got worse.

"Spake your vame, narlet!" Shad roared.

With a sense of impending disaster Nat stepped up on his end of the log, saying: "Little John is my name, little—[he dropped his voice at that word, but the audience caught it with another howl]—man. And I desire to cross yon log!"

Shad, according to direction, hauled himself up on his end of the log and immediately the blame log began to shift in its blocks, and he started wobbling precariously, wig-wagging his staff in both hands to reëstablish his center of equilibrium.

"Fffff-fine," he stammered desperately. "Bbbb-but fff-first let's joust a bit!"

Joust heck! It was all either of them could do to maintain his balance on the side-rolling log. Purely by accident the left end of Shad's staff swung around and fetched Nat a good one on the right hip. Shad snatched and grabbed at the pole and the other end came slicing around and caught Nat on the left shoulder. Nat lost his temper and let Shad have one in the stomach with the end of his staff, and Shad said *"Oooff!"* and what little balance he had left went south. Shad started side-running on the log, all in the same spot, his left hand taking mighty grabs at the empty air for support and finding none, and all at once over he went and 260-some pounds landed in the tub of water.

A silvery wave of water sprang up like a tree covered with ice and descended upon Nat with a splashing crash, and then his balance shattered and he went over backward and prat-first into the tub and on top of Shad, and the high end of his staff caught in the backdrop and the whole thing came down over their heads and engulfed them in splashing, wet, shouting darkness.

By now the audience was half crazy. Some of them had laughed so much they were kicking around on the floor wailing "*My stomach! My stomach!* My sides are splitting!" One man had a heart attack and another laughed himself into a stroke, and still it didn't stop because now part of the backdrop had come into contact with the footlights and the tallow candles started eating it up, and all at once and to his utmost horror Nat heard Benny's muffled voice crying: "Fire! Fire! the giddy backdrop is afire!"

Thrashing, slipping, shoving at the smothering backdrop (which was like fighting a pillow—punch it here, it pops out there), Nat blundered into Shad in the darkness.

"What news?" Shad wanted to know.

"Look out, you fathead! I want out of here!"

"*You* want out! *You* want out!" Shad bellowed. "What a you think *I* want to do? Cook myself in here like a potato in its jacket?"

Then, on hands and knees, he finally found a triangular opening in the backdrop and heaved it up, shouting: "Me first! Me first!" His burly, tousled head emerged just in time to catch a bucket of water flush in the face from that energetic self-appointed fireman Benny.

"*Blaugh!*" Shad roared, spitting water and blue words all

covered with water, and by this time the man who had been having the heart attack had already had it and somehow lived through it, while the fellow who had laughed himself into a stroke was trying to explain to the rest of them that he thought the left side of him was paralyzed, but none of them could hear him because by now they all looked as if they had had strokes or fits or something.

The curtain, somehow, came down on the jousting scene between Robin Hood and Little John.

Benny departed for the night beside himself with joy. He had the comic hit of the century on his hands. All he needed was for Shad to show up every night, and twice on Saturday, and go through the same madcap performance he had just presented, and Benny would be able to retire within two years, buy himself a plantation in Virginia, plus a raft of slaves, and live like a Southern gentleman for the rest of his life.

Shad—needing a place to spend the night—had been strangely reticent about the proposal. He had given a noncommittal grunt in answer to Benny's urgent entreaties.

"You fellas always live like this?" Shad wanted to know, after everyone else had cleared out and he and Nat had the little theater to themselves. His question had an incredulous tone.

Nat grinned. "It's never been quite as frantic as tonight. But this has been the way I've lived all my life. My parents were actors, and I was born backstage." He paused, staring into the middle distance.

"My parents were both carried off by the pox in 'sixty-three. Benny and the rest of the troupe have taken care of me ever since."

Shad looked at him soberly for a moment. Then he said:

"Makes us alike in a way, Nat. I never even knew my folks. Senecas got 'em when I was a babe. Senecas brought me up, part way. I'm blood brother to the Laurel Ridgers; that's a tribe down in Pennsylvany."

Shad, Nat discovered, hadn't been boasting when he'd said he was a friend of George Washington's. Nat was interested; everyone had heard of the famous militia colonel. Everyone seemed to like him too: patriot, loyalist, even the English held him in great respect.

"Shucks yes," Shad said. "Me'n' Georgie started the French'n' Injun War together, down in Jumonville's Glen. Then we fought together at Fort Necessity a month later. And the next year we come back with Braddock——"

"You were at Braddock's massacre, Shad?" Nat marveled.

The huge fellow nodded, his face grim.

"Yeah. Me'n' Georgie—we took our lickin' there."

Nat could see that the old battle was still a sore spot with Shad, so he switched away from it. "What have you been doing in Boston?"

Shad became animated. "Well, I tolt the Committee I wanted to stick around till something busted open, and Sam Adams and Hancock and that Dr. Warren said they'd fix me up. So they put me to work under this here Revere fella. You know Paul? Well, he's got a batch a fellas workin' for him—agents, they're called. And I'm one of 'em! We mosey around town and we listen and look, and what we hear'n' see we tote back to Revere and he passes it on to Warren, who passes it on to Adams and Hancock."

"I see," Nat said. "Revere is a sort of clearing house for military information. But look, Shad, I've heard some pretty mean tales told about Adams and Hancock. What kind of men are they, really?"

Shad pawed at his beefy face. "What have you heard—
that Hancock's a smuggler?"

"Well, it's true enough, isn't it? He was convicted, and
the court placed a one hundred thousand pound fine on him.
And the Loyalists say that if he can't overthrow the King's
government, he'll be tossed into quod; that it's a case of
rebellion or prison for him."

Shad nodded. "Yes, and I suppose you heard about
Adams too, eh? How he was made tax collector of Boston,
and got kicked out of his job because he couldn't account
for ten thousand pounds he'd supposedly collected?"

"Yes, I've heard."

Shad shrugged. "Natty, when you're my age you'll understand that people ain't never what they are believed to be,
that the best of us make mistakes. Sure, Hancock was a
smuggler. Just like half the folk along the Eastern coast.
And why? 'Cause there ain't no other way to beat the im-
port and export taxes that fat old King is forever placin' on
us, that's why. Free trade, that's all we want! But that
fatboy king won't give it to us.

"And Adams? Well, in the last ten years Adams must
have held twenty jobs; and he's lost every one of 'em. All
right, so the Loyalists call him a thief; but out of those
twenty jobs what does he have for it? Nothing. He's as
broke as you or me. Where's all the money he's supposed to
have stolt?" He hunched forward on his stool.

"I'll tell you, Natty. I wouldn't give a hoot in Hades if
Hancock was the biggest smuggler and Adams the greatest
thief in America! That ain't what's important about those
men. The important thing is that they got the guts to speak
their minds out when they see that something is wrong. And
people *listen* to them! Because they got that certain some-

thing that draws folks to 'em like a magnet. Folks need a leader, Nat; they always have. Folks need somebody to stir 'em up. And that's what Adams and Hancock are—rabble-rousers. And if they can talk peawits like you'n' me into fightin' for our independence, then I say let 'em go to it!"

Nat looked at his new friend speculatively.

"Shad, is that why you're willing to fight for independence—because an Adams or a Hancock talked you into it?"

Shad pawed at his face and glanced at his sweaty reflection in the makeup mirror, almost with a look of embarrassment.

"Well, no, it ain't. But then I ain't like most folk. Most folk warn't with me'n' Georgie when we fought for our land agin the French'n' Injuns. I got a stake in this here land, Natty. I lost friends because of it. Their blood is in it, like tap roots. Ain't no European king gonna take that away from me!"

Nat looked at himself in the mirror, thinking: *I wish I could have been there with him. I wish I'd had friends like that.*

Nat had a cot in the dressing room, and Shad said that was all right: he'd sleep on the floor with a blanket, because, by grab, he'd slept on much worse in his time. So they blew out the fish-oil burning lamp and settled down for the night. But not for long.

About midnight they heard the alley door slam and then the tramp of boots coming backstage toward the dressing room. Nat sat up and struck a tinder and got one of the lamps going again.

Ralston Morbes, slim and elegant in tight-fitting black, stood in the doorway with his walking stick, surveying them with cold, hostile eyes. He was a weakly, handsome man with about as much warmth and friendliness as an iceberg.

He liked to affect the airs of a romantic man of mystery.

"So," he said to Nat acidly, "you finally found a way to accomplish your purpose, eh?"

"What are you talking about, Ral?"

"You know well what I'm talking about! I've just come from seeing that prize nitwit Benny at the inn. He says I'm through. He says this fat bumpkin here is replacing me. And he says I have *you* to thank for it, as the bumpkin is your friend."

Shad sat up and blinked at Ralston like a sleepy baby. Then he rubbed his eyes and looked again. Ralston returned the look frigidly.

"Did he say fat bumpkin?" Shad asked Nat.

"Yes. Listen, Ral, what happened between you and Benny has nothing to do with me. I merely brought my friend here tonight and——"

"Save your lame excuses, Towne," Ralston snapped. "I'm not in the slightest interested. I don't need this tuppence job! I don't need any of you. Pack of ungrateful rebels; I should have washed my hands of you long ago. I have my own friends!"

"Are you sure he said *fat* bumpkin?" Shad persisted.

"Yes," Nat said distractedly. "Ral, if you'd——"

"That's what I thought he said," Shad muttered. "I just wanted to make sure, because it makes a difference." He rubbed at his moist face and blew out his breath and hauled himself up from the floor.

Ralston struck a sophisticated pose, leaning negligently on his stick. He studied Shad with arctic distaste.

Shad hulked toward him. "You're a mighty pretty man," he commented. "But your mouth ain't so pretty. Something ort a be done about it. You hadn't ort a go about callin' folks fat."

Ralston raised his stick and jabbed Shad's expansive middle with the end of it. "Stand your distance, my man. Or I'll break this over your stupid thick head."

Shad blinked at the stick planted in his navel.

"You say you want that stick broke, brother?" He removed the cane from Ralston's hand as though he were taking it from a baby. Then, holding it in both hands, he snapped it in two like a matchstick—not over his knee: just between his hands, in midair. He tossed the pieces over his shoulders and started lumbering toward Ralston again like a huge, trained walking bear.

Ralston lost his poise. He fell back a step.

"Stand away! Keep away from me, you great sweaty beast!"

Shad reached out with his left, caught up some of the black finery covering Ralston's chest, and yanked the elegant actor in close to him, seemingly all in one quick, effortless movement.

Nat left his cot. "Shad! Don't hurt him."

Shad looked back at him with a shocked expression.

"Hurt him? My goodness, Natty, I ain't about to *hurt* the poor skinny fella. All I was fixin' to do was reset the slant of his hat."

He caught the brim of Ralston's buckled hat in both hands and yanked straight down—Ralston's head popping through the crown like a jack-in-a-box—saying: "There. Now that didn't hurt him none, did it? Then I was planning on spinning him about like this——"

He struck Ralston's right shoulder with his flat hand, and Ralston, as helpless as a top, spun into an abrupt about-face, and Shad caught him by the scruff of the neck and the seat of the pants, saying: "Then I was going to walk him backstage, somewhat like this——"

Nat, following, would have sworn that Ralston's kicking feet never once touched the floor.

"—till I found one a them buckets Benny uses for fires," Shad continued, stopping by a row of filled buckets and picking up one of them and upsetting it with an appalling splash of water over Ralston's head.

"Then I was gonna turn him just so and aim him for the alley door and give him a little start on his way, like this——"

He planted a huge booted foot in Ralston's backside and propelled the helpless, drenched, bucket-headed man toward the door. Ralston, all arms and legs and no visible head, collided against the closed door, the bucket flying off, and collapsed in a soggy, dizzy heap on the floor. Shad rubbed his hands together energetically.

"Now you see? That's all I was gonna do. I wasn't thinkin' to hurt him for a minute!"

The bedraggled, outraged actor lurched to his feet, got the door partway open, and clung to it as though for support. His eyes were no longer cold. They had the glassy hot look of a starved tiger.

"You'll pay!" he hissed. "Every one of you rebels will pay. And I'll be there on the day of reckoning. Towne, you hear? I promise you—*I'll be there!*"

He slammed the door. He was gone. Shad shook his burly head and sighed. "Fella like that's just as fancy-lookin' as sugar. But I bet he could be mighty mean with a knife—if your back was turned."

Which reminded Nat of the dead man in the alley. They returned to the dressing room to study the powder horn. It was just an ordinary cow horn reconverted to hold powder.

They emptied the powder out, and that didn't tell them anything. Then Shad gave the horn a shake.

"Something still in there." So they broke the horn open.

They found a small, tightly rolled piece of birchbark. Shad grunted and carefully unrolled the strip of bark. To Nat, the hieroglyphic-like inscription it bore meant less than Latin.

"Injun," Shad muttered. "I can read Mingo like you'd read a tavern notice, but this ain't Mingo." Then, perusing the strip closely, he said *"Hmm!"* and *"Huh!"* and finally *"Ha!"*

"Look here, Natty. See that word? 'Androscoggins.' That's an Abenaki word. Tell you what. We got a fella on the committee, Jessie Greene, who's made a study of Injun lingo. He keeps a wholesale winery at the foot of Hancock's Wharf, and we been meeting Revere there in secret lately. I could take it over to him and see what he thinks it is."

Nat hesitated. "I promised that man I wouldn't let anybody else have it."

Shad nodded understandingly. "Sure. Well, I'll just slip over there tomorrow morning and see the boys, tell 'em about it. You can't tell: it might just be something important."

Nat cut the greasy rawhide thong from the horn and attached it to the roll of birchbark, then looped it about his neck and shoved it inside his shirt.

Yes, he thought. Important enough that a man killed to get it, and a man died to keep it.

3

I DON'T MIND DYING, BUT...

The house was packed the next night. Even the aisles were jammed. It was Standing Room Only. And once again the famous jousting scene between Robin Hood and Little John was a howling success. Benny was in a hysteria of happiness; he was forever attempting to throw his spindly arms about Shad to give him brotherly hugs . . . and Shad was forever giving him hasty, brotherly, straight-armed shoves away.

Benny's only worry concerned the expense of burning up a fresh backdrop every night (and two on Saturday); and Nat's and Shad's only worry concerned the unpleasant possibility of not escaping in time from under the burning backdrop some night.

After the show Nat and Shad sat before the tarnished mirror to remove their greasepaint, and Shad said: "Jessie and the other boys want to see you and that birchbark you got. We can skip over there right now. There's a mob fight going on over to the Common, and we ain't likely to run afoul of no patrol tonight."

Nat paused for a moment, staring at his grease-sheened

34

reflection in the mirror. In a way he was a little doubtful of becoming personally involved in the hotbed of Boston politics. In another way he was impulsively glad, excited. But one way or another it seemed inexorable—and had been ever since he had unwittingly darted into that alleyway off Tremont Street.

"All right," he said simply.

Greene's warehouse had the damp, heady odor of brick walls long submerged in wine. The square façade was dark and shuttered for the night. It seemed to bear the somber aspect of a business building brooding over the wistful memory of old, happy, by-gone commercial days, as if watching a ghostly parade of long-gone customers coming and going. But then all the mercantile houses in Boston bore the same scar, ever since Gage's Port Act.

Shad gave a tricky knock on the heavy slab door, and a minute later the spark of an eye appeared at the peephole.

A hoarse voice seemed to issue from the eye. "The word?"

"Doc," Shad said.

"Doc who?"

"Oh for grab's sake! Doc Warren, that's who! You bent-headed old coot! Now open up! Who do I look like to you —Lord Rawdon?"

The eye winked away with a throaty chuckle. Shad grinned at Nat.

"That's Ed Norton, Jessie's head clerk. He's a great one for passwords and secret signs and all that hocus-pocus."

The door swung open, and they stepped into tomblike darkness. Nat jumped when he suddenly heard the hoarse voice right at his shoulder.

"The Committee is waiting for you in the cellar, Shadrach."

"Shadrach?" Nat repeated. He heard Shad clear his throat.

"Ed, if I could just see you, I'd take you by the ears and ankles and pull you inside out and see how you looked hoppin' about on your nose!" The disembodied Ed chuckled at Nat's side, and gave Nat a nudge in the ribs.

"That's why I ain't about to strike a light, Shad," he said.

"Is Shadrach really your name?" Nat asked.

"Well, what did you think it was—*Shadow?*" Shad fumed.

Mutely they stumbled along a narrow blind corridor to a door which opened to the pale glow of a slush lamp on a shelf. Ed—seventy years old if he was a day, as bald as a new-born baby, with a hooked, red-veined nose which suggested that it was his habit to sample every keg of wine received by the establishment—picked up the lamp and led them down a flight of breakneck stairs to a cellar so dank and malodorous that Nat wanted to turn around and go upstairs again.

You couldn't see the walls for the barrels barrels barrels of spirits. French wines, Spanish wines, Italian wines, rum from the Caribbean, brandy from New Orleans, African Madeira . . . you could get befuddled just from looking at it, let alone smelling it.

A cluster of men were sitting around a small table bearing a burning whale-oil lantern. They were pawing through a clutter of maps, and a blue-gray smoke coiled voluptuously over their heads as they puff-puffed contemplatively at their clay pipes.

"Paul," Shad called. "This here's Nat Towne I tolt you about."

A stocky, pouchy man of about Shad's age, with a greasy smile and excitable eyes, stood up and welcomed Nat with his hand.

"Hi, Nat. Shad says you ran into some trouble last night. But here, meet the boys. This is Billy Dawes, an express rider."

Nat shook hands with a well-setup young fellow who winked at him gaily. Then he met Jessie Greene, the owner of the warehouse: a short, blocky man with a squarelike figure; his head too. He had a bland face and a mild smile and a firm handgrip.

Then there was a dour, lemon-faced man called John Boyd, who handed Nat a damp hand like a limp fish; and Mathew Commings, who right off the bat told Nat he'd been a participant in the Boston Massacre; and Harvey Allen, who wore a thick red beard and who had deserted from His Majesty's navy five years before; and finally, at the head of the table, Doctor Joseph Warren.

He was a moody, handsome man in his early thirties. He had a quiet smile and quiet ways. Lord Rawdon had publicly called him the greatest incendiary in all America, and Nat, frankly, had expected to meet a much more bombastic man.

"What's yer tale, myte?" Allen asked abruptly. " 'Oo was the cove what got done in in the alley last night?"

"I don't know," Nat told them. "He was in deerskins, I know that. And he had this powder horn Shad's told you about."

"And you never saw the assailant?" Warren asked.

"No, sir. Not to be able to recognize him again. He was just a shape in the dark."

"May I see the roll of birchbark now?" Jessie Greene suggested.

Nat removed it from his neck and handed it over. Anticipatively, the Patriots—except Warren, who remained seated and calmly smoking—gathered around Jessie Greene as he unrolled the strip of bark and placed it under the lantern-light.

"It's Abenaki, right enough. Unfortunately, I'm not as well versed in the language as I am with the Western dialects. Let's see . . . as near as I can make out it is a message from some of the important sachems of the Androscoggin and Kennebec tribes, intended for the Seneca Nation."

"Then it must be from Paul Higgins," Warren suggested.

Jessie nodded, muttering to himself as he traced his finger down the bark strip. Nat looked at Shad. "Who's Higgins?" he whispered.

"Chief of the Androscoggins. White boy the Abenakis stole and raised. Some call him a renegade."

Jessie looked up and tapped the strip. "I gather that this is an answer to a Seneca question. I believe that the Senecas must've asked the Abenakis which side they would fight on in the event of a war between the British and the Americans."

Warren removed his pipe from his mouth and leaned forward.

"And the answer?"

Jessie shook his head. "As I say, I'm a little vague—but it looks as though the Abenakis think they'll fight for the British."

The men around Jessie straightened up slowly. No one

said anything for a moment. Then Billy Dawes yawned and stretched and said: "Which probably means we'll have both Seneca and Abenaki against us if we have to fight the redcoats." It didn't seem to bother him much.

But the possibility obviously bothered the rest of them a great deal; especially Shad, who had fought Indians all his life.

Jessie looked at Nat. "Perhaps we'd better take charge of this message," he suggested. And Warren roused himself, saying:

"Yes. It wouldn't be advantageous for us if that message were to fall into the wrong hands."

"I don't understand, sir," Nat said.

Warren tapped at his lower teeth with the stem of his pipe.

"Simply this: it would jeopardize our cause if the Senecas were to learn that the Abenakis were ready and willing to fight us. It would probably influence the Senecas into taking the same step."

"But they're bound to learn sooner or later."

Warren smiled a small reticent smile. "As you say, Nat— *later*, in this case, will suit us far better than sooner."

Nat hesitated, conscious of their eyes upon him. Then he tucked in his mouth and reached for the birchbark.

"I'll see that it doesn't fall into the wrong hands. But—I think I'd better keep it. You see, I gave my promise I would."

They seemed to understand that. A promise to a dying man was considered a sacred thing.

"Just be very, very careful with it, Nat," Jessie warned.

"Don't worry, Jess," Shad said heavily. "If anybody tries to get it away from him, I'll bust their arm for 'em."

The meeting seemed to have reached its conclusion. The Committeemen were knocking out their pipes and arising from the table, and Ed Norton went for the slush lamp to light their way upstairs.

"By the by, Nat," Dr. Warren said, touching Nat's arm with his pipestem. "How would you like to join our group? I believe Paul could always use another man. Correct, Paul?"

"Right, Doctor. Can't get enough of 'em. Right now information's our biggest weapon."

Again Nat hesitated. Now—still a part of the inexorable pattern—he was faced with the decision. He met Warren's steady gaze.

"Doctor, do you think it will come to fighting—war?"

Warren looked down at his pipe, speculatively, as though he half thought to discover something more than just dead ashes in the bowl.

"Yes," he said finally, "I believe it will." Then he looked up at Nat. "Are you afraid of fighting, Nat? Of being killed?"

"Yes, sir, I sure am," Nat said candidly.

Warren smiled quietly. "So am I, frankly. I don't mind dying, but I'm deathly afraid of being killed."

"How's that, Doc?" Shad looked bewildered.

"To die of sickness or old age, of natural causes, holds no horror for me," Warren explained. "But to be killed by a bayonet or a musket ball . . . " He shrugged, and knocked out his pipe in the palm of his hand.

"But if it comes to fighting," Nat prompted, "you'll still go through with it?"

"Yes, I will, Nat," the doctor said simply.

Nat nodded. "All right, Doctor. So will I."

4

THEY BOTH KNEW THEY WERE TALKING ABOUT DEATH

Shad was in a fever to get away from the theater right after the show the following night. He barely bothered to remove the grease paint from his face, saying:

"Something's up, don't ask me what. But Harvey Allen just sent word that Warren wants me quicker than a starvin' man wants a meal!"

"Well, what about me?" Nat wanted to know.

Shad was already to the door. "Beats me, Natty. But if I was you, I'd scoot over to Jessie's just as soon as you finished here. See you!"

Nat cleaned himself, switched to his street clothes, grabbed his hat, and hurried from the dressing room. He bumped into Benny in the wings. The manager was toting a fat bag of clinking coins, and he started cooing ecstatically like a mother over her first-born.

"A fortune, Nathaniel, dear lad! A veritable fortune! Remind me to consider doubling your wages and presenting a bonus to Shad—some day."

"All right, Benny. I'm in a hurry now. See you to-morrow."

He'd never been more wrong in his life. A sergeant from the Fourth (King's Own) Regiment was tacking a fresh proclamation onto the billboard in front of the theater. The date it bore was April 18, 1775.

Ed Norton let him into the warehouse. The old fellow was so excited he kept plucking at Nat's sleeve all the way down the corridor.

"What's up, Ed?"

"Big doings. The regulars are going out!"

"Out? You mean out of Boston? To where?"

"Concord, you idiot! Where else?"

"Well, what's about Concord?"

"Gunpowder!" Ed cried. "That's what about Concord! For months our boys have been raiding the King's stores, and they've made a military depository in Concord. Why, child, Concord's full of cartridge paper, flints, musket balls, bombs, fuses, spades, kettles, billhooks, swords, *and* powder!"

"And Gage knows it?"

"Bless you, to be sure he does! His Tory spies know everything. And what's more, he aims to get it! And I mean *tonight!*"

Nat left old Ed at the door and started down the steps on his own, only to have to step aside as a nameless stranger came hurrying up the stairs. The man gave him a quick sideways look and a fleeting grin in passing.

"Some excitement, eh bucko?"

"I reckon," Nat agreed. And then the man was gone and Nat went downstairs.

Billy Dawes and Dr. Warren were alone for the moment,

both standing, bending over the table, studying a map. Billy looked up and grinned.

"Hear the news, Nat-o?"

"Yes. Is it true?"

Warren reached for his pipe absently, still staring at the map.

"Very true. One of Paul's men, Jasper, a gunsmith, heard about the intended movement this afternoon from a British sergeant. Gage planned to make this a secret expedition— but there's one thing no general has ever been able to do, and that's keep a soldier's mouth shut."

"Colonel Smith of the Tenth Foot, and Major Pitcairn of the marines are taking the grenadier and light infantry companies," Billy said. "We figure there'll be about seven hundred men in the detachment."

You had to hand it to Revere's agents, Nat marveled. They really kept their eyes and ears cocked.

And later, much later, he had to marvel at the vagaries of history. Somehow, in legends, Revere was to emerge as the hero of the night. Actually Warren had already sent out about a dozen riders to warn the countryside and arouse the minutemen and the militia. And Shad had been one of them. Now Warren looked up at Nat.

"Are you at all acquainted with the countryside, Nat?"

Nat had to confess that he wasn't. The doctor merely nodded, glancing back at his map.

"Billy and Paul are going to ride direct to Lexington to warn Adams and Hancock—it's very possible that Smith will attempt to place them under arrest. Then they'll continue on to Concord.

"There are two main roads leading to Concord. One by way of the Neck toward Roxbury, then around to Cambridge and Menotomy, and so on through Lexington. This

is much the longer road, and I'm going to send Billy along
it, because Paul seems to be rather tardy arriving tonight."
He looked at Nat again.

"Will you go with Billy? There might be patrols out. If
one man is stopped the other might still get through."

"Yes, sir. I'd like to." Next to Shad, Nat didn't know of
anyone he'd rather join in a night of adventure. Billy was a
casually courageous young character who had recently made
a name for himself when he had beaten a British soldier
silly for insulting his pretty wife. Billy grinned and slapped
Nat on the shoulder.

"All right, Nat-o! Let's see if you can make a horse
move!"

"Nat," Warren suddenly called. "I have a feeling that this
is the moment we were talking about last night."

Nat stared at the older man, the recognized intellectual
head of the Committee of Safety.

"All right, Doctor. I guess it can only happen to us once."

Warren nodded. "That's right. No matter how bad it is—
only once."

They both knew they were talking about death.

Nat was on a roan liberally sprinkled with gray pepper.
Billy had a horse so coal-black it would probably shine
purple-blue in the sun. The two mounts went *plok-plok*
nonchalantly down the road to Boston Neck. Billy kept
standing in his stirrups to peer ahead into the gloom. As
impulsively inclined as he was for action and excitement, he
was, on the other hand, not foolhardy. He knew when to
bide his time.

A platoon of soldiers was slowly filing over the Neck
some distance ahead of them. Nat saw Billy's teeth flash in
the dark.

"Turn your hat, Nat," he said, doing so to his own. "Cock it like an officer's lid. You're an actor, ain't you? Well, now's the time to strut your stuff. We're going to mingle with those soldiers like we were officers. God willing, we'll elude the guard at the blockhouse and cross over with the redcoats."

The big thing in their favor was the pitchy darkness of the spring night. Nat reset his hat on his head at an aggressive angle and spurred the roan into the lead.

He was a pretty good mime for his time, and he'd had two months in which to study the mannerisms and affectations of British officers. He put the roan to a canter and came loping in among the platoon of foot soldiers, heedless of their safety, shouting:

"Gad's life! Whose ragamuffin squad is this? Don't you dolts know enough to clear the road for a general officer? I say, you there, Leftenant! Plague take it, man, I mean *you*! Cawn't you move your beastly guttersnipes aside? Cawn't you recognize Lord Percy when you see him? Deuced stupid of you, if I do say so!"

All in a dither, the luckless lieutenant and the Neck guards shouting at them, the foot soldiers tumbled frantically aside into a general disorder in the dark, as Billy Dawes—his hat cocked, his right hand akimbo on his hip, disdainfully tall and ramrod-straight in his saddle—came *jinglety-bump, jinglety-bump* through the tumult; out-Percying Percy for all he was worth.

"Majaw!" he snapped at Nat's silhouette, "get that leftenant's name. Put the blightaw on report, what?"

But Nat, bigheartedly, elected to give the bamboozled lieutenant a break and merely called back: "Carry on, Leftenant. A trifle more alertness and respect the next time, what?"

And then the two of them were pounding down the road one after the other, the eight hoofs of the horses going *thup-thuppity-thup!*

Nat pulled alongside Billy to shout: "Which way is Revere going?"

"The short way! Across the Charlestown Neck!"

"Hope he has the luck we just had!"

Billy's grin flashed in the moony night.

"If he ever gets started! He has to go through no end of nonsense about hanging lanterns in the North Church steeple!"

"What for?"

"Beats the nathun out of me! That's Paul's way. He's afraid he won't be able to get across the Charles River, and the lanterns will warn a Colonel Conant in Charlestown that he and his pals had better take off for Concord in Paul's place!"

The moon was successfully breaking through the cloud-strung April night as Billy and Nat came pounding into Roxbury, and Billy—grinning as usual—looked back and called: "Let's really rouse 'em, Nat-o! Let's get these fat farmers out of their warm beds and into their fields with something besides plows and spades for a change!"

"All right, let's go, old boy!" Nat yelled.

And so they came banging down the main street whooping like demented Shawnees on a dawn attack. *"HEEE-YAH-YAH-YAH-Yaaaah!"*

"UP! Every fat farmer's son of you—UP! Turn out! Turn out! Grab your firelocks! You rabbly rebels! The regulars are coming out!

"EEEE-YU-YU-YU-Yuuuu!"

The night flowed by them, ghostly with the grotesque stark attitude of the leafless trees. The wind of their own headlong passage blew chill upon their faces, knifing through their jackets and shirts and trembling their blood. The pale road wound on ahead of them, through the damp salt swamps, moist and cold and moon-struck.

Then they were galloping through Brookline and scalp-yelling again and waving their hats and spurring the horses on on and on.

"The regulars are coming out! On to Lexington and Concord!"

They saw lights light up, small bright squares set in the large black squares of the looming houses. Windows and shutters were shot aside and nightcapped heads appeared; and once, fleetingly, Nat saw a woman step back behind her husband leaning at the window and put her hands to her face. And he thought: *They know. The women always seem to know when it's going to be bad.* Because it was probably something in them, in their nature or blood—a hangover from their cave-dwelling ancestors, when their menfolk had gone out with a club in their mighty fists to face a savage enemy, and had never returned.

He looked at Billy Dawes humping and hunched and flying before him and thought: *Billy—good luck to you, old boy, tomorrow.*

Then they were going *pam-a-pam-a-pamma* across the Charles River bridge and slicing a noisy passage through sleeping Cambridge.

"EEEE-Yuuuu! Up! Up! Everybody up! The regulars are coming out!"

The coming-to-life town fell in their pulsating wake, and now they were going pell-mell down the lonely road to Menotomy and the road was so hard under those sure-flying hoofs that Nat could feel the slam of it all the way up his backbone and he exulted in the jarring, rhythmic sensation

of inexorable motion. As yet they hadn't encountered a
single patrol, and it looked as though their luck was in.

There was activity in Menotomy. Lights were ablaze in
the homes and there was a bustle of movement around the
dooryards.

"*Eee-YAH!*" Billy cried. "The regulars are coming out!"

A tousled head popped through an upper window and an
irate voice shouted: "We know it! How many times you
gonna tell us?"

Billy looked back at Nat. "Guess Paul's already been
through here!"

Or someone, Nat thought. Because by now Colonel
Conant and others were spreading the alarm far and wide
across eastern Massachusetts. At Lynn and Billerica and
Acton, at Woburn and Reading and Danvers, at Tewksbury
and Andover and Pepperell and Worcester, farmers were
tumbling out of their beds to reach for muskets issued in
King George's War thirty years before or for fowling pieces
or blunderbusses—any excuse for a gun that would fire any
excuse for ammunition.

It was half past midnight when Nat and Billy galloped
into Lexington. The town had been aroused, and Parson
Clarke's home bore the festive aspect of a public house.
They dismounted and went by a well-lathered horse to the
door, where an excited militiaman on guard greeted them.

"Heard the news?" he asked, only too eager to tell them.

"No," Billy said. "What?"

"The regulars are coming out!"

Billy dropped his jaw and clasped his hands, turning to
Nat with a look of horror. "Did you hear *that*? The regulars
are coming out!"

"Do tell," Nat said, and they went by the bewildered
guard, laughing.

Paul was toasting his feet at the fireplace. His face was a polished rose with firelight and sweat. He beamed at his two friends.

"Hello, Billy! Hi, Nat. You boys have any trouble? Let me tell you what happened to me at Medford. Got jumped by a British patrol! Yessir! Two of 'em, mounted and waiting for me in the middle of the road. So I had to miss Cambridge and double back to Medford like I had the devil on my tail! Did you get Cambridge, Billy?"

"Yeah. Where's Adams and Hancock?"

Paul jerked a thumb over his shoulder. "Packing up their papers. They're going to spend the night in the swamp. I been waiting here for you for half an hour."

Nat was going to ask him why he hadn't gone on to warn Concord, but just then a bluff-faced man somewhere in his fifties, entered from another room with his wig awry and with papers clutched in both hands. He gave Billy a harassed smile and glanced curiously at Nat.

"This is Nat Towne, Sam. One of my boys. He rode with Billy tonight," Paul said.

Sam Adams transferred the papers in his right hand to his left and offered his right to Nat. "Are you going on to Concord tonight?"

"Yes, sir," Nat said. "Quick as we can."

Adams nodded, a look of abstract dissatisfaction on his bluff face.

"I've waited years for this moment—and now when it's finally come, John and I have to run and hide in some stinking swamp like cravens."

Nat supposed that Adams was referring to the well-known fact that General Gage had been quite willing to extend amnesty to all the Patriots *except* Adams and Hancock. Those two firebrands he had sworn to conduct to

England in chains. That was the trouble with being the figurehead of any revolutionary attempt: you were always the target.

"Well," Paul said, clumping for the door, "we'd best get along."

Nat looked back at Sam Adams. Was he a great man, or was he a rogue and a thief who talked other men into fighting for him? Nat had no way of knowing, and it didn't really matter. The thing had started now, and Adams had become a symbol of the snowballing; for that he deserved respect.

"Goodby, sir," Nat said.

Adams, looking at them soberly, nodded. "Good luck, gentlemen."

The three riders started down the road, Revere now in the lead. All at once Billy called: "Hi! Hold up, Paul. Somebody's coming!"

Nat reined in and put a hand on the cantel to turn back in his saddle. He could hear the *thuppity-thup* of hoofs chopping the road.

"Think it's a patrol?" Paul asked anxiously.

Billy shook his head. "No. Just one man. I can see him now."

A solitary rider materialized out of the gloom and made a smooth transition from canter to walk with his mount. In the moonlight they could see that he was a young gentleman dressed to the nines in his Sunday best. He halted before them, touching his hatbrim jauntily with one finger.

"Good evening, gentlemen! I understand the regulars are coming out. I'm Doctor Samuel Prescott from Concord. I'm just now returning home from a—uh call I made in Lexington."

Billy grinned at the young doctor. "By draggit, Doc, it's a heck of an hour to have to tend a patient."

Dr. Prescott coughed decorously behind his hand. "Well uh—to tell the truth it wasn't quite a patient I was calling upon."

Paul chuckled. "Don't stop now, Doc. This is just getting good!"

The doctor laughed good-naturedly. "I confess you've caught me out. I was visiting my fiancée. A Mistress Millikan—a very proper young lady, I might add, even though the hour is now quite late."

"Care to join us, Doctor?" Nat offered. "We're on our way to rouse Concord."

The doctor, it seemed, was young enough to still be romantically restless. "A capital suggestion!" he said. "It sounds exhilarating. My Concord patients are forever getting *me* up at all hours of the night, and now I have the opportunity of paying them back! Onward, gentlemen!"

Paul and the doctor in the lead, the four-man troop went *bumpity-bump, bumpity-bump* down the shadow-flickering road, down to a turn-off where the Hartwell farm sat crouching back from the road.

Right out of nowhere two British officers sprang before them with a flash of swords.

"Halt, you rebels, or we'll blow the bally lot of you to Kingdom come!" And one of them went *ta-wee—ta-wee* on a whistle, and instantly two more redcoats emerged from a field bordering the road.

"Go it, Nat-o!" Billy cried, and he wheeled his horse into a sharp oblique and booted home the spurs.

"*YAH!*" Nat roared, and he humped over and went booting after Billy, sweeping by Prescott's off side—and the doctor must have been mounted on the horse of horses, because it took off from practically a dead halt and caught up to Nat within three bounds.

Now the two regulars in the field were smack before them, and Nat caught the long brittle-bright glint of their raised bayonets. He swerved right, nearly colliding with Billy's near side, and shot a look across his shoulder to see Prescott lashing his way through the scrambling, shouting soldiers with his whip. Then he looked ahead and saw the black ragged line of a stone wall rushing to meet him and heard Billy yell: "All together now!"

Then he felt the bunch and gather of the roan's barrel between his legs and the sudden gut-grabbing lift as he went up up into the star-streaming night . . . but something was wrong, very wrong, because when Billy said "all together," he hadn't meant all on top of each other. But they were, or nearly so, and that's the way they tried to go over that blame wall: Nat's right stirrup hooking with Billy's left, and Billy himself tilting over against Nat's shoulder as the blackness of the sod field sprang up at them.

And then an absolute nothing for a suspended moment: no pain, no shock, no realization of what had happened to them—spilling together, and striking the solid black loam so hard that they saw only stars that didn't belong to the night but only existed behind their knocked-silly eyes.

Nat rolled over, hearing a multitude of hoofbeats pounding everywhere at once, and pawed at his eyes to rake the swirling stars from them. He felt Billy grip his right arm.

"Hi! Nat-o! Lookit old Doc go! Cannon balls couldn't catch him!"

Straight across the moony field, the hoofs kicking back black clods, the doctor was hunkered down and winging on like a hurricane, the horse (undoubtedly the horse of horses) reaching, throwing, going, getting out of there.

That was the ride. And not one of those who had started

out from Boston ever reached Concord. History had decided to brush its shoulder with a pretty young miss called
Millikan, and that night her sweetheart would "pay back"
his Concord patients.

Nat and Billy crawled to the far end of the stone wall,
where it fell into a crumbling pile, and into an azalea
thicket. They looked across the field and at the moon-bright
road. Paul had evidently tried to ride for a nearby copse of
wood but had been captured by six more regulars who had
been in hiding there.

Now they had him in the road and were questioning him.
A Major Mitchell was in charge of the patrol, and he wasn't
being very nice about it. He clapped a pistol to the side of
Paul's head.

"Who are you?"

"Paul Revere."

"Well, isn't that wonderful! So we've caught the famous Revere, have we? The bully boy of the Sons of Liberty. *Paugh!* I've seen better looking parodies of a man on Guy Fawkes Day! What are you up to? Answer quick, or by Jove, I'll put daylight 'tween your waxy ears!"

"Rousing the countryside," Paul said. "Every town for miles around has been alarmed, and five hundred men are assembling at Lexington."

"Why is he telling them that, for goshsake?" Nat whispered.

"Good old Paul," Billy whispered back. "He can't help boasting."

But the boast served a useful purpose, for just at that moment they all heard the distant *pam-pam* of alarm guns from somewhere to the east. The regulars started looking around at the surrounding darkness apprehensively.

They held a greatly agitated council and finally decided to get on their way. They actually had no authority to place Paul under arrest, so they told him he was free to go— without his horse, which they commandeered.

Nat and Billy waited until the road was vacant and then they came out of hiding and started walking back to Lexington, hoping to overtake Revere. But they never did. By the time they reached the town, Paul had already departed from Parson Clarke's house in a chaise with Adams and Hancock. A passing militiaman told them that the trio had taken off for Burlington.

It was now after two o'clock.

It was the morning of April 19.

5

LET IT BEGIN HERE!

Captain Jonas Parker of Lexington had called out his militia, and he had 130 of them collected on the village green. They were known as the minutemen, a term which actually dated back to 1756 when a company of Massachusetts soldiers called themselves "minnit" men.

They had been standing around in the open cold for more than an hour when Nat entered the Green, and—with no more news coming—Parker had just dismissed them with the order that they were to return immediately at the sound of the drum. About half of them were heading for their homes, while the rest made a beeline for Buckman's Tavern.

Nat accosted the captain. "Pardon me, sir. I'm Nat Towne. I made the ride with Billy Dawes from Boston to——"

"Who in hopping Hades is Billy Dawes?" Parker snapped. He was an impatient man with a great deal on his mind.

"He works for Paul Revere, who——"

"Oh? Well, where in the name of goodness is Revere

now? He's been screaming for action for five years, and now when we have it, where is he? Is he going to face the red-coats with us or not?"

"I don't know, Captain. That's what I wanted to see you about. I want to join you, but I don't have a gun." If you are going to do a thing, Nat had decided, then do it all the way.

"Well, what am I supposed to do—grab one out of the air? I don't have enough guns for the men I've got. And on top of that some fat monster just came to town and beat up two of my men and stole their muskets and now has himself barricaded in a house with them."

"Why would he do a thing like that?"

"How do I know! Because he's a fool! A big barrel-bodied beast of a man with a face like a tomato and a mouth like a wounded bull!"

Nat's attention perked up. "You happen to know his name, sir?"

"Well, I should hope the whole town knows it by now! He's been shouting it like a bugle—about how he's Shad Holly from Pennsylvania and how he's come up here to show us Massachusetts mule-heads how to fight a war. I'm only afraid he'll get some of my men so riled they'll decide to burn down the house to get him out."

Nat took the directions to the house in question and set off at a run. The place was a tidy, two-storied frame affair, and a sergeant and six minutemen were standing out in the road pegging rocks at it—and also insults. All of the front windows had been broken, and every so often a lantern or bottle or even a marble clock would come flying out of one of them and scatter the men in the road.

"Sergeant," Nat said, "that's a friend of mine in there. Let me talk to him, will you?"

The sergeant had nearly worked himself into apoplexy. He could hardly talk for furious wheezing.

"*Talk to him! Talk to him! Shoot* the dad-gasted fat cow, you mean!"

"Brother!" Shad's voice bellowed from an upper window, "I heard that! And when I get my hands on———"

"Shad!" Nat yelled. "Shut up and come down and unlock that door!"

"Natty? By juckies, boy, what're you doin' here? Holt on a minute. Just wait till I come tell you about these here Lexington folks. Natty, you just won't believe what kind a peewits they got in this colony!"

A minute later the front door swung open and Shad, big, beefy, bombastic as all get out, stepped onto the porch bearing two muskets.

"What news?" he cried, grinning.

With a furious rumble the minutemen started to surge forward.

"Hold on, can't you?" Nat yelled. "Let me talk to him. Shad, what's this ruckus you've got yourself into?"

Shad put both muskets in one huge paw and swiped at his moist face with the other. "Natty, I didn't do nothin' at all, hardly. I'm as innocent as the day I was bornt. After I near to run my nag to death tryin' to wake up these mush-headed Mess-achew-setters, I come hot-footin' over here 'cause I figure this is where the fightin's gonna be. And right off the bat I run into these two molassesmen, or whatever they call themselves.

"They're headin' away from the Green, see? So I says to 'em: 'Brother, where you off to?' And right now they get snotty about it and tell me to mind my fat business. Fat, that's what they said. And they said they weren't about to

get themselves kilt tryin' to stop a thousand or some lobsterbacks, so they was goin' home and hide under their beds.
Well, I said, 'That's all right, brother, if you ain't got no
guts, you can't help it. But just gimme the loan a them
muskits of yorn, 'cause I aim to get me some redcoats.'

"But they don't wanta, see? They're afeered some little
girl might jump out at 'em from the bushes on their way
home, and they'll need them muskits to fight her off with.
And right then's when I stumbled."

"Stumbled? What do you mean stumbled?"

"What I said. I accidental-like stumbled and fell against
the one fella and he went flyin' into the other fella and they
both went down and I lost my balance and fell on top of
'em, and my goodness, you never heard such swearin'! So I
had to shut 'em up, didn't I? I couldn't have 'em kickin' up
all that naughty talk right here in a public street, could I?
Then these other bezabors here come beltin' down the street
and don't give me no chance to explain what I was tryin' to
do with those two brave molassesmen."

Nat looked at the sergeant, and the sergeant cleared his
throat and went *tsk* at a chipped tooth and shrugged.

"Guess we was chasin' the wrong fella," he said apolo-
getically. "Guess we should have gone after those cowardly
blame deserters. Sorry, Holly. You did say your name was
Holly, didn't you?"

"That's what I said, brother." Shad took Nat's arm and
moved him away as easily as if he were moving a chessman
on a board.

"Here, Natty, take one a these muskits. I also got a
couple of powder horns and shot bags. I tell you, though: I
never seen such a place as this Mess-achew-set. You know
they ain't got a single *rifle* in the whole country?"

Nat hefted the gun and threw it up to his shoulder to take aim. It was a twelve-pound Tower musket, known as the Brown Bess. The crazy thing didn't even have a rear sight. But he said nothing; he didn't believe in looking a gift horse in the mouth. Abruptly they heard the *Ddddrr-rum-rum-rmmm* of the drum, and an alarm gun went off.

"Let's go!" Shad cried. "It's starting!"

It was four-thirty. A rider called Thaddeus Bowman had brought the news. The British were right behind him. Pitcairn was leading a vanguard of six light companies.

In the chill dark the minutemen were pouring from the tavern and from their homes. A bedlam was created: shouts of "Well, but I ain't *got* no gun!" "Are we gonna get ammunition or ain't we?" "Some of you fellas standing around there trot over to the meeting house! They got a supply of powder'n' ball there!" "Jimmy! Hey, who's seen that fool Jimmy!" were heard.

Uniforms, of course, were nonexistent. Homespun was the order of the day, and some of it had been spun so long ago that not a few of the minutemen looked like ragmen. And you could take your pick when it came to ages, starting at fourteen and working up to around seventy. The young boys looked eagerly frightened; the older men looked nervously angry. Nat couldn't imagine how he looked. He knew how his stomach felt though. Like a cold cannon ball.

If it doesn't happen soon, he thought, *I'm going to throw up.*

He looked at Shad, who calmly poured a palmful of powder down the barrel of his Brown Bess, followed that with a piece of paper wadding, then dumped in five-six buckshot, a musket ball, and another wad of paper, next tamped the whole mess home with his ramrod, then rapped the stock sharply with the heel of his hand to knock powder into the pan, and finally pushed forward a section of the lock, setting the frizzen. The entire operation had taken him about fifteen seconds.

"I could do it faster if we had paper cartridges," he told Nat. "You know anything about guns, Natty?"

"Nothing—except what I just saw you do. I think I followed it."

"Nothin' to it. Just be draggit sure there ain't no sparks left in the barrel from your last shot. She'll blow fingers off your mitt if there is. Sometimes she'll hang fire after you pull the trigger. Also watch that your flint don't get worn, else it won't spark, and that the powder in the pan don't get damp, and that the touchhole ain't stopped up. Wish we had us some Pennsylvany rifles," he added in a sincere mutter.

The Green was a triangle formed by three roads. The Boston-Concord road was its base, and Parker lined up his men about a hundred yards from this thoroughfare. Nat finished loading his musket and looked around. There were maybe seventy armed men in the line. That was all. Seventy against seven hundred.

He swallowed a mouthful of saliva that felt like a lump of lead. And that was the last saliva his mouth held for a long long time.

Shad was on his left and a little scrawny fellow of about sixty on his right. Ten or so down the line he saw Billy Dawes wave to him gaily. "Paul's back!" Billy called.

"Where?"

Billy jerked a thumb over his shoulder. "Watching us from Buckman's upstairs. Hancock sent him back for some papers."

Nat looked at Shad, who shrugged and said: "He ain't got no gun."

The sun rose leisurely on a cold clear day and sent a sharp east wind ahead of its light. Then they saw the first of the redcoats, marching stately in precise, rhythmical order, vivid in red and white, their forest of bayonets aglint. A faintheart took one look and said:

"There's so few of us. It's stupid to stand here!"

Parker said: "I'll shoot the first man who tries to run." Nat had an idea he meant it.

Major Pitcairn, so handsome he was almost pretty, rode forward and coldly surveyed the Americans' token line of defense. Then he ordered his men into battle position. The regulars in the rear ranks trotted forward with the accustomed "Hurrah!" and fell into line with those in front, forming three deep in two sections.

Almost as if without a will of their own, some of the minutemen began to pull back, slowly. A few of them actually drifted off to the sidelines, trailing their muskets as inconspicuously as possible.

Parker looked around and called: "Stand your ground! Don't fire unless they do! But if they want to have a war, let it begin here!"

Pitcairn, accompanied by two other officers, rode forward on their magnificent mounts to within thirty yards of the Yankees. The major was the enigma of the British army. He was actually liked by his men; even more astonishing, the Boston patriots also liked him.

"Don't be a fool, man!" he called to Parker. "Lay down your arms and disperse! If you do—I promise you we won't fire!"

Parker hesitated. The hopelessness of the situation was

cryingly obvious. Someone muttered: "C'mon, Jonas. Do what he says, afore we all get ourselves killed!"

But Parker didn't want to. He wasn't the sort of man that had it in him to crawfish. He hungfire, indecisively, even though some of his men were starting to draw back and melt away. They weren't, however, obeying Pitcairn's instructions. They were taking their muskets with them.

The Major raised in his stirrups. "Lay down your arms!" he shouted. "Why don't you lay down your arms?"

Nat glanced up at Shad. The big fellow's mouth was tucked in tight and he was holding his musket at the ready. He wasn't about to pull back until ordered to. The little old man at Nat's right nudged him.

"What're you gonna do, boy?"

"I'm gonna wait, like my friend."

The little man gulped and said, "Me too—I guess."

"You rebels!" one of the British officers cried. "We'll have your arms if we have to take them!"

And right then someone—and no one then or now or ever will know who—fired the shot that was heard around the world, and started (aside from the war) an argument that would go on and on forever. The English claiming "You fired it," and the Americans affirming "No, you did," even though it was already too late to matter who the nameless, faceless, countryless, trigger-happy man was. It was all a part of the inexorable pattern, and the shot—whether British, whether Yankee—simply had to be fired.

One of the lesser British officers panicked—so completely, in fact, he forgot he wasn't in charge of the advance guard.

"Fire! By gad! Fire!"

A volley went *KA-BALOWM!* from the British left section. But it was jerked and from the hip and went high, and Pitcairn with a stunned look, turned and snatched for his sword and swept it downward, crying:

"Cease fire! *Cease fire!*"

But Parker had been hit and he stumbled back into Billy Dawes' arms, yelling: "Fire!"

Shad's musket whipped up and went *Plam!* And then Nat's, then the little fellow next to him, and finally a scattered volley. But it was feeble at best. The minutemen were pulling back.

Pitcairn's horse reared with a double graze, and a regular in the front rank dropped his musket, put his hands to his stomach, said something no one could understand, and went headlong into the road.

The British second volley tore into the retreating Americans, and eighteen men went down, and eight of them would never get up again.

Pitcairn couldn't do a thing. The same thing that had happened five years before at the Boston Massacre was happening again: the regulars were caught up in the vortex of action and they were so wild they couldn't hear his or any officer's orders. They fired at will, then leveled their bayonets at the hip and charged.

"Make tracks, Natty!" Shad grabbed Nat by the arm. "I seen a lobsterback baynet charge afore. There ain't *nothin'* can stop 'em!"

Nat was only too ready to go. He saw that long dazzling line of bayonets coming, and everything that was in him and loved life and the preservation of life said: *Let's get out of here!* He turned and started to run, but paused within twenty yards and looked back, and what he saw he would carry with him till his dying day, because it was his first brush with what he was to experience many times later, and it was so vivid it imprinted itself in his brain as though it had been stamped in purple ink.

Parker, alone among his dead, wounded in the hip and down on one knee, still refused to withdraw. The British came glinting toward him as he was reloading. He piled the ramrod home, then threw it aside and started to bring his musket up as the picket-work of British bayonets cut him down.

He simply disappeared beneath the redcoated, steel-bright charge . . . a man who would rather be chopped to ribbons than retreat an inch.

Nat winced and started automatically to turn back, muttering: "No no no, you filthy lobsterbacked——"

But Shad had him by the arm and was pulling him along, stumbling and lurching and faltering across the Green.

"Don't be a dad-gasted fool! *Nat!* You hear me? We ain't done yet! By grabbit, boy! We're just startin'!"

6

SEEMS LIKE WE GOT ENOUGH PEOPLE BLEEDIN' ALONG THIS ROAD TODAY

Nat tried to match Shad's rhythmical, easy-going Indian trot down the road to Concord. He never would have dreamed that a man as heavy as Shad could have maintained such a pace; but Shad told him he could keep it up all day if he had to.

About a mile or so out of Concord they ran smack into the three small companies of the Concord militia, reinforced by a fourth company from nearby Lincoln. They totaled about 150 men, and they were on their way to see what was doing at Lexington.

A Captain David Brown called: "What news?"

Shad stopped and blinked. "Say, that's my line," he complained.

Nat stepped off to the side of the road and sat down on a rock to try to get back his wind. The trouble with war, he decided, was that you never got any sleep. He had now been on his feet and in the saddle for twenty-four hours.

There were four captains in charge of the militia, and when they heard from Shad what had happened at Lexington they each wanted to do something different. Brown was in favor of holding the road against the British, a suggestion which made Shad paw at his sweaty face energetically.

"Cap," he said, "that idee ain't worth a tinker's dam. A hunnerd'n fifty farmers ain't about to stop seven hunnerd regulars. We just tried it at Lex, remember? Now if you'll listen to me———"

"Why should we listen to you?" a Captain Miles wanted to know. "You don't even come from around here, that I know of. What makes you a military strategist?"

Shad blew out his breath gustily. "Listen, brother, I fought at Jumonville's Glen with Washington, and at Fort Necessity with Washington, and at Braddock's Field with Washington. I was fightin' French regulars and Mingo savages while your Pa was still marchin' you to the woodshed for a taste of his strap for sassin' your Ma. And just an hour ago—while you was rollin' over in bed and wishin' the rooster wouldn't make so much fuss—*I* was fightin' off British muskets'n' baynets with nothin' but sticks'n' stones'n' naughty words for weapons! Are you gonna stand there and tell *me* about war, brother?"

The four militia officers were staring up at the huge Pennsylvanian with rapt attention. Then Brown said: "You've actually fought under Washington? *George* Washington?"

There it was again, Nat realized. Americans everywhere had heard of Washington, and they always seemed to brighten up at any mention of his name.

"Looky here," Shad said briskly, "you expect reinforcements, huh?" And, when they answered "yes, soon," he said: "All right, then let's fall back and take up position on them hills you got around your town and wait for the rest of the militia to back us up. What the Mingos done to Braddock twenty years ago, we can do to old Smith today."

All at once a tall farmer yelled, "Hi! Here they come!"

Nat sprang up and looked down the road. A solid wedge of crimson and white and glittering steel was cutting through the avid green of the woods. To the simple townsmen of Concord it must have seemed like the grandest army Europe had ever produced—and in a sense it was.

The four militia officers looked, blanched, and swung into accord. They decided to adopt Shad's plan.

"COMM-*panies!* About face! Forward . . . *harch!*"

Nat and Shad fell in with the rear guard. Someone up ahead started a *rat-ta-ta-tat-tat* on a drum, and a fife began to squeal like a pig stuck under a fence. Five hundred yards behind them the British started to thump their drums and blow their fifes. War, in tuneful step, was coming to Concord.

First the road curved along the base of a long narrow ridge; then it ran into the little town and through it and swung right, passing a second hill; then it crossed the North Bridge over the Concord River and took off for a third hill called Punkatasset. A fifth company of militia, Captain George Minot's alarm company of old men and young boys, had been stationed earlier on the first ridge.

Shad shook his head. "You got to consollydate your forces," he told Brown. "Ain't no good havin' thirty men on one hill and forty on the next and so on. One redcoat baynet charge agin a hill like that will leave you nothin' but weepin' widows and wailin' mothers."

So Minot's company was called down from the ridge, and all the Yankees withdrew to the second hill overlooking the North Bridge.

Colonel Smith wasn't entirely simple-minded. As soon as he saw that first ridge, he eyed it with dubious suspicion and ordered Pitcairn to throw out the light infantry as flankers to clear the way—just as Shad had predicted. Finding the hill deserted, Smith then proceeded to march his army unmolested into Concord.

There was sudden activity on the second hill. Nat looked around and saw a man in an actual uniform coming through the laurels. This was Colonel James Barrett, who was in command of the district militia.

"What about our stores, Colonel?" Captain Miles asked anxiously.

"Everything's been taken care of," the colonel assured him. "We've hidden the powder in the woods, and buried our cannons and muskets in the fields." Then he stared down at the seemingly endless procession of redcoats filing into the town and frowned darkly.

"I don't like this. If they send troops across the bridge, we'll find ourselves flanked on this hill. I think we'd better pull back to Punkatasset Hill."

So the Yankees retreated for the third time and took up a ragged position on Punkatasset to wait for reinforcements, which weren't long in coming. Captain Isaac Davis brought two companies of militia from Acton, and John Moore ushered in a raft of minutemen from Bedford, and from everywhere unattached volunteers were heading for Punkatasset Hill. The American force was suddenly three or four hundred strong.

Nat remembered that he had never reloaded his musket

since the fracas at Lexington and he set about doing it. That cold cannonball feeling was rolling back into his stomach again as he watched the boys and men and old granddaddies making their way up the hill. There was going to be trouble —fighting and dying trouble; he could feel it coming like something preparing to leap out of a nightmare.

Down in the town Colonel Smith and his staff officers were refreshing themselves in the taverns, while the grenadiers began to search the 25 or so houses for the powder and arms. A Captain Laurie had been stationed to guard the North Bridge with three companies of infantry.

The grenadiers were finding precious little for their pains. They uncovered two small cannons, which they dismantled, and 500 pounds of musket balls, which they threw into the millpond. When Barrett saw that happen he merely grunted, stating: "We can dredge those up after they leave."

Next the British rolled a hundred barrels of flour into the pond, and quite a few of the thrifty Yankees began to grumble at such wanton waste. But Shad said: "I seen that happen afore. The outer flour swells and protects the rest. You won't lose much."

Abruptly the courthouse and blacksmith shop took fire, and that really bugged the iron-eyed men watching from the hill. All the officers got into a hassle about what should be done. Some advocated patience and caution, while others, firebrands, wanted to march smack into Concord and defend it or die in the attempt.

"Come on, Jim. Are you going to let them burn the blame town down?" Joe Hosmer, the adjutant, demanded of Barrett.

No, Barrett didn't want to see Concord burnt, but he

didn't want to see a couple of hundred farmboys cut to ribbons either. Finally he turned to Major Buttrick.

"All right, John. March 'em down there. But don't start anything. Don't fire unless fired upon."

Two fifers started to shrill The White Cockade, and a drum went *dddrump-tump-tumm!* Shad heaved himself up from the ground, growling.

"C'mon, Natty. We might as well tag along. They're going about this here business all wrong, but I reckon we got a help 'em at it."

Nat raised himself on his musket. The cannonball feeling had left his stomach at last. Now he could feel little icebergs floating around in there, bump bump bumping together.

Captain Laurie saw the armed farmers coming and he pressed his panic button. He hurriedly sent a messenger to Colonel Smith for reinforcements. And it was then that Smith made his first big mistake of the day. He decided to lead the reinforcement companies himself; but being a huge, fat, slow man (and not for a moment believing that Laurie's three companies of regulars couldn't stop a rabble of hayfoot farmers), he came clipping along as fast as a turtle with the gout.

Nervously Laurie withdrew his men to the east end of the bridge, ordering a detail to take up the planks so that the Yankees couldn't cross. Shad, as big and burly and belligerent as a bull, shoved himself up front and shook his musket at the regulars.

"Hi! You lobsterbacked leather heads! Put them planks back! Don't you peewits know that's public property you're smashin' up?"

To Nat's utter amazement the detail of regulars actually did stop lifting the planks. They hurried back to their ranks on the townside of the bridge.

Laurie—obviously an officer who wasn't worth a hoot in a pinch—arranged his men in a hysteria of haste, blundering by placing his three companies one behind the other so that only the front company could fire. Major Buttrick led his little army up to the foot of the bridge and halted them. The Americans and the British stared at each other across the span.

It might have been a stand-off—except for Laurie. He lost his head and ordered a volley. The British were rattled, and their first fire was ragged, mostly dropping shots that went *toonk, toonk* in the water; except one bullet that clipped by Captain Brown's ear.

"Why, gol dummit! They're firing *ball!*"

"What'd you think they'd fire—*bean*bags?" Shad yelled.

The British fired a second disorganized volley, but with better elevation, and one of the Yankee fifers fell with a wound in his side, and Captain Isaac Davis jumped like a hit rabbit and went down dead, and an Acton man was dead before he struck the ground, and two others slumped into the road and started kicking.

Major Buttrick went out of his mind with fury.

"Fire, boys! By holy hector, give it to 'em!"

Nat caught his breath and swung up his musket and the Yankee volley tore into the facing company of redcoats, and twelve British soldiers went down. It was enough for Laurie—for his men too. They wheeled about and retreated into town without any semblance of order.

The Americans were baffled by what they had just done. They had stood up to British fire, answered it in unison,

bowled over twelve redcoats, and chased three companies
of regulars away. They were stunned by their own audacity
and achievement.

Slowly, almost hesitantly, they crossed the bridge and
stepped carefully around the British dead and wounded. No
one seemed to know what to do. The officers argued with
each other, the men argued with the officers, and those from
Bedford argued with those from Westford who argued with
those from Acton who argued with those from Lincoln,
while the Concord men shouted: "Whose town *is* it, anyway?"

So some wanted to push after the British, some wanted
to wait right there, others wanted to return to Punkatasset
Hill, and a few said: "Let's go bury Davis and Hosmer."
And in the end everyone seemed to do just about what he
felt like doing. Not quite two hundred men remained
together on the east side of the bridge, seeking cover behind
a stone wall. They weren't quite certain just what it was they
were waiting for, but they waited for it anyhow.

Disgustedly Shad slouched over to a birch tree and
parked his huge self in the shade. Nat hunkered down
beside him and started reloading.

"Tell you something, Natty. What we done here today
ain't gonna mean a dang thing lessn these here Yankees
learn how to get together and follow up their advantage. I
never seen such obstinate, independent fellas! I wish I could
turn Washington loose on 'em for just one week!"

Nat was staring at the British dead in the bright sunny
dust of the road. It was a weird thing, death was. One
moment you're standing in a road—breathing, thinking,
hearing, smelling, seeing, just as you've always been doing.
And the next moment *Blam-o!* Nothing. Dead. And stran-

gers were stepping over you cautiously. And you couldn't know about it. And you couldn't care less.

"But it's not their fault, Shad," he said, shaking his mood. "These Yankees aren't like you Southerners. You fellas have been fighting Indians, or each other, since 1607. The first thing your Dad hands you when you're old enough to reach is a rifle gun. I'll bet half of these farmboys never even fired a gun before today."

"Ain't that what I'm sayin'?" Shad demanded. "They need *trainin'*! They need *discipline*! They need a general officer who won't take no nonsense offn 'em! They——" He broke off abruptly to indicate a tall, gangly boy of sixteen who was upending his powderhorn over his grandaddy-type fowling piece.

"Now looky there at that pore nutmeg-headed idjut, fixin' to blow both hands plus half his nose off at the first shot! Hi! Boy! You with the sleepy look on your stupid face! That ain't no cannon you're shovelin' powder into, you know!"

While the British prepared to start their retreat to Boston, and while the Americans stalled indecisively, Shad—pretending to be angrier than he actually was—gave a lesson in powder charges to a gang of bewildered looking farmboys.

He tore a shingle of bark loose from the birch tree, set it on the ground, selected a musket ball from his warbag and placed it on the piece of bark, then tilted his powder horn over the ball and let it pour until he had just enough to cover the ball completely.

"Now you farmboys do the same thing. Then pour that amount of powder into the palm of your hand and study it till you know by sight just how much to use for each charge."

Fifteen minutes later, as more and more minutemen and militia came hurrying toward Concord from the surrounding district, Shad and Nat struck northward across a field called Great Meadow, Shad mumbling to himself: "By draggit, I bet four Mingo braves and a Catawaba squaw could whale the tar outn these here mule-brained Yankee hayseeds!"

But Nat noticed that Shad kept glancing surreptitiously at little clusters of farmboys who were busy peeling bark from trees to practice the lesson he had taught them, and he rather imagined that Shad was secretly proud of "those there mule-brained Yankee hayseeds."

A mile out of Concord a lone house stood at a place called Meriam's Corner, and it was there that the strangest battle of the long, drawn-out war that had started that morning began. Nat and Shad joined hundreds of militiamen who were filtering through the orchards, all heading toward Meriam's house. Out on the road Nat saw the crimson smear and silver sparkle of the retreating British army.

Colonel Smith had thrown out flanking parties on either side of the road, and, without warning, a squad of them suddenly turned and fired a volley at the Americans who were starting to press in. Again they jerked their triggers and pulled high and harmless, the bullets humming overhead and snicking through the leaves.

"HI-YI!" Shad screeched like a savage and popped his musket, and a redcoat twisted grotesquely and went down. Then Nat and the rest started to fire and one-two-three soldiers more fell into the road.

Eagerly, dodging from tree to tree, moving up toward the stone walls that bordered the road, the Americans pressed forward, fired, reloaded, ran on ahead, still keeping under cover, and took up fresh positions and fired again.

To the British it seemed as if rebels were coming down from the clouds. There were nearly a thousand Yankees lining the road by now, and more on the way all the time. They fired from the windows and roofs of houses, from behind barns and trees and walls, and many of them—in their anger—simply stood in the open fields and cracked away.

The redcoats dropped dropped dropped. The dead were left behind; the wounded became walking wounded. The scarlet column began to lose its sense of cohesion. It straggled, broke, regrouped; it stumbled over bodies. In parts it paused and fired and then lurched on.

The Yankees ran on ahead, dodging, skirting, firing, reloading . . . .

But it wasn't another Braddock's massacre. The British flankers who were well back from the road saw to that. Nat got caught with eight men from Reading as they trotted up to a stone wall close by the road and crouched down to fire.

Nat started to level his musket over the wall when the boy next to him threw up his gun, arched his back like a drawn bow and tipped right on over in that position. Something went *whock!* against the wall at Nat's left elbow and he pivoted on his heels and saw a strung-out squad of flankers coming behind them.

"Look out! They're behind us!" he yelled, and went ducking out of there, the *pak! pak! pak!* of Tower muskets chasing after him.

All along the road the Yankees were becoming cognizant of the fact that they were being hit from behind. Somewhere off on his left Nat heard Shad's bawling voice.

"Git away from them walls, you dad-gasted bumpkins! Don't let them flankers shoot you in the *back!*"

Still, many of them—in their hot excitement or cold fury or just plain bullheadedness—forgot about the flankers and continued to press up to the walls. And paid for it.

Slowly, miserably, fiercely, the disorganized redcoat column blundered into Lexington and began to disintegrate as a fighting unit. Small groups (gangs, actually) of soldiers began ransacking houses and taverns. Fat old Smith, beside himself with outrage and amazement, tried to form a rearguard to hold back the Yankees. But it was a waste of time, because the way the Yankees had themselves deployed, Smith needed not only a *rear*guard but a right and left and forward guard as well. He was simply surrounded; and—just to keep him good and frustrated—a Yankee sharpshooter, or maybe just a lucky-shot Yankee, put a musket ball through his fat leg for him.

Going at the rear of a pile of rails in a running crouch, Nat fell in with a batch of men from a town bearing the remarkable name of Billerica, and they prepared to make an ambuscade on Major Pitcairn.

"Who's got some powder, for grab's sake?" he wanted to know. "My horn's empty."

But he wasn't the only one. In fact many of the provincials that day came to fight along the road only as long as it took to use up their powder. Then they said "to heck with it," and shouldered their empty muskets and went home to their chores.

A rangy looking backwoodsman in buckskin (with an honest-to-gosh rifle in his tanned capable hands) turned and handed Nat a skinning knife that must have been twelve inches long from butt of hilt to point of blade, saying:

"I'm near dry mysilf, boy. See what you kin do with this."

Nat didn't know what he could do with it. He sure didn't want to go up against a bayonet with it. But he said: "Thanks, friend."

"Here they come!" a rat-faced man with mad eyes hissed. "Pitcairn's on the hoss. He's mine. You fellas bust up the gang behint him."

The Billerica men leveled their muskets over the parapet of rails, as Nat raised his head for a look and saw Pitcairn leading a platoon of grenadiers toward the ambuscade.

"Pour hit home!" the rat-faced man cried.

KA-BAL-LAL-LAM! A blast of fire exploded from the pile of rails, and the grenadiers turned this way, that way, paused, turned halfway back, and then started to drop. The major's horse reared, throwing the unhit officer to the ground, then bolted. It leaped a wall and came right at the pile of rails.

Nat dropped the skinning knife and sprang out from behind the ambuscade, calling: "Whoa boy! Whoa! Easy, beauty!"

He grabbed for the reins, caught them, and stroked the lathered horse's neck, gentling him. Then he removed the major's pistols from the holsters, and a powder flask plus a bag of pistol balls from the saddlebag. He felt like a fighting man again.

"Scoo, boy!" he shouted, and slapped at the horse's rump with one of the pistol barrels. The horse got out of there like a shot.

The British retreat staggered out of Lexington, with the Yankee muskets still *plam-plam-plamming* at them. If the provincials had had any sort of cohesion at all they could have stopped Smith cold right there at Lexington Green. But they were even more disorganized than the British.

Militia, minutemen, unattached volunteers were all scrambled together; two Chelmsford men with four Framingham men, and a Stow officer with three Sudbury men, and nothing made any sense at all; no coherence, no plan of purpose, just multitudes of fighting-mad individuals on their own.

Nat, straggling behind as he tried to estimate the proper amount of powder to charge a pistol, found the road littered with the droppings of war: grenadier caps and Tower muskets and cartouche boxes and powder flasks and water bottles. Dead men too. But not all of them.

A wounded corporal was propped against a stone wall. He had been hit in the leg and left behind. He stared at Nat for a static moment as if to determine the extent of his ferocity, then pointed to a canteen that was ten feet away in the road.

"Give us a sup, Reb. I'd do as much for you."

"Sure," Nat said, fetching the soldier the drink. "Hurt much?"

"Nar. I've 'ad worse. I'll live—if yer bloody friends down't scalp me."

"We're not savages. We'll take care of you. Say, Corporal, can you tell me how much powder to use in a pistol?"

"So you can shoot down more of my mytes? Not bloody likely!"

Nat nodded and started away. The corporal called after him.

"S'y! Thanks for the drink, Yankee!"

War's a funny thing, he thought as he hurried down the road. *We kill each other, yet we're not bad men—most of us. And none of this would be necessary, if they would just leave us alone!*

General Gage had anticipated the need of a relief column for Smith's expedition, but for some reason (how stupid can you be?) the orders were addressed to Major Pitcairn and sent to his quarters, and there they sat because Pitcairn was already long gone to Concord. When this glaring blunder was finally realized, Gage ordered Brigadier General Percy to Smith's relief with 1,000 men and two six-pound field-pieces. Because of the mixup, Lord Percy didn't get on the road until 9:00 A.M. This delay nearly proved fatal to Smith and his battered regulars.

It was after 2:00 P.M. when Percy and Smith finally came together on the road near Menotomy.

This combined British force was an impressive, even for-midable, sight, and for a while the Americans began to hang back—long enough for Smith's men to catch their breath under the cover of Percy's muskets. At three-thirty the retreat was resumed.

The situation was getting badly out of hand by the time Nat caught up with the Americans. The regulars were bound and determined to get something out of this bloody day's work, and so they began to break ranks to enter and loot all the roadside houses they passed. Lord Percy gave no order against these depredations, his intent being to pay the Americans back by terrorizing the countryside.

But instead of experiencing terror, the irate Yankees turned wild-eyed with hate. They came pressing through the trees and up to the walls again, firing and reloading like fiends. And more and more of them were coming all the time, until finally there were 2,000 of them fighting from tree to tree, house to house. And that's the way the British and the Yankees came to Menotomy.

From a mortally wounded elderly country gentleman

(who knew all about horses and hounds, foxes and fowling pieces) Nat had learned how to charge his pistols, and he arrived just at the height of the fighting.

What he saw as he came through a pear orchard would stay with him like a bill of notice posted on every lamppost of every street he would ever walk. Many Yankees had taken cover in Menotomy's houses to snipe at the invaders, and the British in retaliation had charged these abodes, bayoneted all the inhabitants, plundered the household goods, and set the houses on fire. The Yankees went berserk with rage.

Later, when he heard from stay-at-homes who had been nowhere near the battle how the Americans had only fought at a safe distance from behind the shelter of trees and walls, Nat wanted to hit somebody. Because in Menotomy these angry, vengeful, hating, hot-blooded Americans came wading into the road in clots to meet the British face to face.

There they stood firing, loading, swearing blue murder at the redcoated invaders who were despoiling their land, knowing (they *must* have known) that the soldiers would cut them down. And they did. And it was clubbed muskets against bayonets. And the farmers went down in the road cursing and hating and dying, refusing to back off.

Forty Americans fell in Menotomy. But they took forty British with them.

A horseman was coming through the trees, and wherever an American saw him he would pause to yell a hurrah. It was Dr. Warren. He was trying to swing a force against the British rearguard, and he wasn't having much success because Percy had unlimbered his two six-pounders to cover his retreat and the cannons were tearing the Billy-be-diddled out of the orchards.

Warren spotted Nat and swerved his horse in a sharp oblique.

"Towne! Get forward and find General Heath! Tell him to try to turn Percy away from the Charlestown peninsula in Cambridge. If we can catch him on the Charles Bridge, we've got him!"

Nat flapped his hand in response and started off through the trees. Snipers were moving by him on all sides, all with the same open-mouthed, intense look. Then someone yelled: "Lookout! Flankers!" And Nat ducked behind an elm and heard the rattle of musketry around him.

Right in front of him was another of the inevitable stone walls, and he went for it in a crouch and started crawling along it. He was in a more or less open patch of ground, backed by a dense stand of trees.

A glancing sledgehammer blow struck his right shoulder and threw him face against the wall. He gasped and gritted his teeth and reached for the pistol in his belt with his left hand, glancing over his right shoulder. He expected to see the British flanker who had shot him coming to finish the job with his bayonet.

But it wasn't a soldier. It was Ralston Morbes.

The Tory actor was only twenty paces away, standing at the hem of the trees with a smirk of evil satisfaction on his darkly handsome face. A smoking dueling pistol was in his hand.

Leaning against the wall, Nat brought up his left hand and snapped a shot as Ralston jumped behind a tree. The bullet went *whock!* into the trunk, and Nat dropped that pistol and took the one he had been holding in his right hand. He could see very clearly just what was going to hap-

pen. Ralston, under cover, was going to reload and pot him as he crouched in the open by the wall.

"COO-WEEGH-HH-HAA!" A gosh-awful shriek came ripping across the clearing and down the corridors among the trees. Nat saw Ralston start away from his covering tree, looking everywhere at once in shocked horror. Abruptly the huge, powder-stained, sweaty figure of Shad Holly burst through the trees and came charging at the Tory with his clubbed musket in his big fist like a stick, looking for all the world like some great demoniac monster let loose to ravage the earth.

Ralston took one quick, wide-eyed look and, whether his pistol was loaded or not, he got out of there and right now, ducking into a laurel thicket and taking off with a terrific smash of noise.

Shad came trotting back to the wall, his face flaming red as he panted for air.

"Blasted Tory twirps! That's the first one I seen skulking along the fringe of the fight. He had a hoss back there in the thicket!"

"That was Ralston Morbes," Nat said, easing himself to a sitting position with his back to the wall. His arm felt sticky.

"Was it? I thought he seemed familiar. 'Course I would've knowed him right off if he'd been wearin' a bucket on his head. Bushwhacked you, eh? Here, lemme see." The big fellow hunkered down and started pawing at Nat's wet shoulder.

"My goodness, Natty. I hope that Ralston could play Robin better'n he could shoot—else Benny must a had a terrible show on his hands! Holy Hector, boy, he didn't give you nothin' more'n a bee sting."

"Shad, you mind telling me what that yell was you cut loose? I never heard anything like it in my life."

"You didn't? By juckies, where I come from we use Injuns to wake us up in the mornin' instead a roosters. That there was my Caughnawaga war cry. Tuneful, ain't it? It always turns green farmers white. Here, I got something for that flea bite of yorn."

He rooted in his war bag and came up with a silver-scrolled flask, unstoppered it, gave the neck a sniff, then gave himself a swallow of the contents, said *YAH!* and poured it liberally over Nat's nicked shoulder, saying: "Helps stop the bleeding. From the taste of it 'twould help stop anything. Take a belt. It'll put you on your feet again."

Nat tried it, and it was like swallowing a strand of barbed wire.

"That's French brandy. How'd you come by it?"

"Oh, sorta by accident. That fat old Colonel Smith, you know, he can't take hisself nowhere less he has his batman lug along a whole raft of sweetments and lick-yours and them such comforts. Anyway, as ever'body was haulin' out a Lexington I see this here pore batman strugglin' along under this pack a goodies, and there was five Woburn farmers back in the woods takin' potshots at the pore devil and puttin' no end of holes in the sweetments and lick-yours. So I tolt 'em to stop that nonsense and I went out in the road and said to that batman: 'Brother, lemme give you a hand with that load.' And for some fool reason or other he took one look at me and threw me the whole pack and took off down the road like I'd yelled Boo! at him."

Shad fed himself another strand of bobwire, yelled *EEE-YU!* and replaced the flask in his war bag.

"I got the pack hid out in the woods," he said. "Reckon I'll come back this way someday and dig it up. Gimme a length of your shirt so's I can make you a bandage. Seems like we got enough people bleedin' along this road today."

It was nearly sunset when Lord Percy led his beleaguered troops into Cambridge, still fighting every foot of the way. And, as Warren had feared, Percy was shrewd enough to switch his intended course. He took the road that ran across the little isthmus that connected the Charlestown peninsula with the mainland.

His wounded and dog-weary men sprawled on the heights of Bunker's and Breed's hills and waited for the Royal Navy to come take them off.

By the time Nat and Shad reached Ploughed Hill, near the Mystic River, the long day's battle was over and the indifferent sun was bidding them all good night.

They were beat to a standstill. They laid down and closed their eyes, and sleep came at them like the dazzle of a bayonet charge. And while they slept there on the hillside, Massachusetts turned over with a groan as if in a death- or perhaps birth-roll. From all over the province hundreds of Loyalists fled their homes and made their way helter-skelter down the darkened, militia-rowdy roads to Boston.

Once Nat awoke briefly and, sensing a phenomenon of movement around him, half sat up and looked across the dark harbor at the great cluster of lights which was Boston. Staring, he experienced a constriction in his chest. The vast dark bowl of the bay was half surrounded by a gigantic U of sparkling fires. Like a dropped necklace the scattered fires flared and faltered, flared again, seemingly intent on encircling Charlestown and Boston with a ring of flame.

A ghostly shadow slouched by his right-hand side, the slant of a musket silhouetted over its shoulder.

"Hi!" Nat called to the man. "Whose fires are those?"

"Milishy!" the shadow voice came back. "Most of us are stayin' here to keep the lobsterbacks'n' Tories penned up in Boston."

"Who gave the order?"

"Beats me, bub! Nobody that I know of. I'm just stayin' because I guess it's the only thing to do."

Nat stretched out on his back again and stared up at a sheeplike drift of stars high high overhead.

I guess it is, he thought before he dozed off again.

7

INTERESTING ARMY WE'RE BUILDING HERE

All through the long, noisy following day the sorry-looking procession of Loyalists filed across Boston Neck, coming in their carts and carriages and wagons, on horse, on foot, suffering in silence the hoots and insults from the hundreds upon hundreds of ragged, rowdy militiamen who lined the main artery to Boston.

Nat, standing beside Shad at the Yankee barricade on Boston Neck, watching the Tory vehicles lumber slowly by, each one heavily overloaded with prized personal possessions, felt a twinge of pity for these suddenly uprooted people. And he said as much to Shad.

The big fellow nearly dropped his musket.

"Sorry for 'em! Did you say *sorry* for 'em? My goodness, Natty, you don't want to go around like a man with an empty grain sack for a head sayin' things like that! Feelin' sorry for a Tory is like feelin' sorry for a timber rattler after he's gone and bit you in the heel from behint!"

"But, Shad, these people are Americans too. Most every one of them was born right in this country like us."

A grubby idler standing by Shad's elbow turned a smirking face up at Nat. "Say, what are you, bub? A gol-dummit Tory lover?"

Shad blinked his eyes as though he couldn't believe he had just heard the interruption. Then he turned and leaned his big moony face down at the grubby man.

"Brother, did I ast you to set your big mouth in my right ear while I was talkin' to my friend? Did I do that?" he demanded.

The grubby man's ferret eyes ran skippingly over Shad's enormous frame, and he swallowed with difficulty.

"No, I reckon you didn't, mister," he admitted.

"Then do us both a favor and take your big mouth somewheres else afore I push it a foot and a half up through your nose." That business finished with, Shad swung back to Nat.

"Naw, Natty, you got it all wrong. There's a re-al big difference atween them Tories and you'n' me. I don't give a cat's backside where an American was bornt. But if he's livin' here in this country, then there's only one a two things he can call hisself. Either he calls hisself an *American*, like you'n' me do—or he calls hisself an Englishman, like them Tory folks do. And startin' from yesterday the time for straddlin' the fence has come to a roarin' halt! From now on a man either says he's an American and he's willing to fight to prove it, or he says he's an egg-suckin' wife-beatin' penny-stealin' Englishman and he's got to get the heck out and stay out!"

A tall, old, tired, sickly looking gentleman in a blue and buff uniform had halted on a handsome sturdy horse directly behind Shad. His hooded invalid eyes studied the big Pennsylvanian for a thoughtful moment. Then he called:

"You there—with the English officer's hat. What's your name?"

"Shad Holly, if it's any a your business," Shad snapped over his shoulder. Then he blinked and turned for a second look, and added, hesitantly: "Sir?"

The sick old officer nodded heavily. "Good man, Holly. Wish I had a hundred of you. Your size and with your ideas." Then he raised a hand to a farmer with a seaman's cutlass stuck in his belt and said: "Carry on, Captain. Let's get these people across the Neck and finish up this business today."

"Say," Shad addressed the captain in charge of checking the Tories through the barricade, "who was that old coot, anyhow?"

"Him? That's General Artemas Ward. He's senior general of the Massachusetts army, and he's just taken command of the cordon we got around Boston. Folks say he didn't want to take the job on account he's as sick as a sailor with the scurvy; but he did because it's only gonna be temporary."

"Yeah? Well, who's gonna end up being Commander-in-Chief, then?"

"Beats me, brother. Some fella they got comin' from somewhere."

A commotion erupted between two carriages that were stopped at the barricade, and the captain turned away to go see about it. A voice greatly thickened by spirits began shouting.

"You hick-fashed farmers, get outa my way! I'm goin' inta Boshton where ever' loyal shub-subject of the King belongs!"

Nat nudged Shad. "By grab!" he whispered. "It's Billy Dawes!"

Shad looked, and a big grin started to spread across his moist face.

"Yeah. And Billy ain't never touched a drop of likker in his life."

The two of them strolled over to the center of the disturbance.

The militia captain was telling Billy he would have to be checked through just like all the other rump-sprung, turn-coated Tories, and that he would have to wait his turn. And Billy was telling him that by grab he was going through *now*, and that no pack of horn-headed rebels had better try to stop him, either!

Shad reached out and caught up Billy by the shirt front.

"So you want a go through, do you, you Tory tarhead? Well, you better and *fast*, else I'll pitch you clean acrost the Neck!"

"Shay, you fat-shized ale keg with legs!" Billy yelled. "You mush-must be lookin' for a bent nosh-nose!"

"*Fat!* Brother, did you say *fat*?" Shad started shaking Billy loose from his teeth. "Well, that does it! I'm takin' you through myself!"

"Wait a minute! Wait a minute!" the militia captain howled. "He's got to be *checked* through. It's orders!"

"Well, ain't that what I'm doin' with him, Cap?" Shad bellowed. "I'm *chuckin'* him through right now!" And he did too, scooping up Billy by the scruff of the neck and the seat of the pants and taking one-two-three fast steps with him and heaving him headlong toward Boston. "Go on, you lousy Tory! Clear out a here!"

The militia cut loose with a roar of laughter as Billy picked himself up, shook his fist at them, and started lurching down the road like a man trying to walk with another man's pair of legs.

So Billy Dawes, the best of Paul Revere's secret agents, went to Boston.

A great unruly army was growing out of the minutemen and the militia and the unattached volunteers. The center—command headquarters—was held by Ward at Cambridge, along with that well-seasoned old French and Indian fighter, General Israel Putnam. The right wing was at Roxbury under the command of General Thomas. The left held the Charlestown Neck, commanded by General Lee. Dr. Warren, Nat and Shad learned as they made their way toward Cambridge, had been appointed a major general.

That was about all they could find out from the multitude of straggling troops they passed on the road. No one knew where Warren was, and Revere was reported to be in Watertown, and someone thought Jessie Greene was still in Boston. Nat and Shad didn't know what to do with themselves.

The road was jammed with sprawling encampments: ratty little tents, backwoods lean-tos, and shoddy hutments that would have given a muddy pig the horrors. Ununiformed men were being drilled by un-uniformed officers. Little earth entrenchments and redoubts were being thrown up and simply named Fort Number One, Fort Number Two, and so on. Connecticut troops were getting into fistfights with Massachusetts troops who were starting brawls with New Hampshire troops who were picking on the poor little Rhode Island troops who were so all-fired scrappy they wanted to lick everyone. It was a lusty place.

Passing through a New Hampshire camp, Shad cast a speculative eye on a homemade flag mounted on a stick and stuck in the ground beside the CO's tent. It looked like a petticoat to Nat.

"Natty, you go on along. I'll catch up to you in a bit," Shad said. "I gotta see a man about something."

Nat didn't get far by himself before a New Hampshire corporal offered him a bite of breakfast, which suited Nat to a T. He dug into a rasher of bacon and three sunny-side-up eggs.

"You a Massachusetter?"

"Nope."

"Connecticutter?"

"Uh-uh."

"Rhode Islanter, then?" Nat shook his head, and the corporal looked baffled. "Well, you ain't from New Hampshire, else you'd already belong to some outfit. Where in blazes *are* you from?"

"Anywhere. Though I was born in Maryland. You see, I used to be an actor before all this started. Actors keep on the move."

The corporal became downright chummy. "Well, look here, then. You don't want to join up with just *any* old outfit, do you? You want a fight alongside the best, don't you? My advice is for you to sign up with us New Hampshirers, 'cause we're right fine folk. You don't want a make the mistake of fallin' in with none of them misbegotten Connecticutters 'cause they're so stingy-mean they're tighter than bark on a tree. Everybody knows that!"

Nat thanked the recruiting corporal and said he'd think it over. Half a mile further along the road a Connecticut sergeant greeted him like a long lost brother and invited him to sit himself for a bite of breakfast, ham and fried potato slices. The sergeant's brotherly advice to Nat was that he should instantly join a Connecticut company, because that way he wouldn't run the risk of getting tangled up with any turnip-stealing New Hampshire outfits.

"What's wrong with 'em?" Nat wondered, letting out a notch in his belt.

"*Wrong with 'em!*" the sergeant roared. "Why ever'body

knows that New Hampshirers is so tight-fisted with a meal or a shilling they're as close as bark on a tree!"

And within ten minutes he was halted again by a fat militia captain who beamed upon him like a benevolent father, saying: "Had your breakfast, young fella?"

Nat thought about it for a moment, then said, "Thanks anyway." But the captain didn't give up. He came over and felt Nat's right arm.

"By nathun! You're a fine strapping lad, you are. Just the sort of man we need to help shift artillery around. Listen, son"—speaking very fatherly now—"this is Gridley's battalion camp of artillery. We're Massachusetts men, we are, and if you'll take a word of advice from me, you'll stop right here before those Connecticut or New Hampshire people can catch you; because, as everybody well knows———"

Nat thanked the captain for the information about all the people who were tighter than bark on a tree and promised to think over his offer. About that time Shad (much thicker about the middle than when Nat had parted from him just half an hour ago) caught up to him.

"What've you got under your coat there?" Nat asked.

Shad blinked. "Where?" And Nat poked his finger into Shad's expansive middle. "There."

"*O-h-h!* There. Why, that there's a lawn petty-coat, Nat. They just ain't nothin' better in the world than lawn to make gun patches outa. Burn off slick as a whistle. Don't leave shred nor spark."

"Shad, did you go and steal that New Hampshire flag?"

"*Steal! Steal!* My goodness, Natty, you ort a know better'n to go along a public road sayin' a terrible word like that! 'Course I didn't steal it. Them Hampshire fellas tried to recruit me with some breakfast; and after I'd had me some bacon'n' ham'n' eggs'n' potatoes'n' a loaf a bread'n' maybe a little mutton and tamped it all down with a quart of ale, I was sort a fullsome and dizzylike when I went to get up, and I accidental stumbled agin their flag and knocked it down in the mud. Well, what could I do? Them fellas being so nice and all? I had to tell 'em I'd wash it up for 'em right away, didn't I? And that's what I aim to do, too." He looked mighty self-righteous about it.

"You mean wash it to make gun patches from," Nat pressed him. But Shad didn't seem to hear him. He was looking on down the road with great interest.

"Looky, Natty. There's that college where all them scholarly-like young fellas come to learn how to yammer Latin at each other, for some reason."

Cambridge had been a pretty little town—before the army overran it. The houses were brick or clapboard with diamond paned and leaded windows. You could see where most of the houses had once sat in little green kingdoms of their own, guarded by tidy squares of white picket fences. But soldiers like to eat, and they like to have a fire to cook their food with, and cookfires call for wood, and there's nothing handier for the purpose than the pickets from a fence, so . . .

A tall, angular captain in a blue militia coat cut across their path, and Shad instantly snapped him a proper salute —which Nat, startled, attempted to copy. Shad, he had noticed, had an infallible quality for spotting a *real* officer: that is, a man who had inherent military skill in his makeup. Most of the officers were pompous country bumpkins, and Shad wouldn't waste the time of day on them.

The captain seemed as surprised as Nat, yet returned the salute neatly. "Yes?" he said. "Can I help you?"

"We're lookin' for General Warren, Captain," Shad told him.

"He isn't in Cambridge right now. He's sending dispatch riders off to all the provinces, telling them what happened at Concord and Lexington. What was it you wanted to see him about?"

Nat gave the captain their names, informing him that they had worked for Warren and Revere as agents before the Concord-Lexington fight. The captain seemed impressed with their history and offered them his hand, stating his own name: Knowlton, Captain Thomas Knowlton of General Putnam's Connecticut regiment.

"Perhaps you had better come along with me," he suggested. "I'm on my way to see Old Put now. He'll know what to do with you."

"Old Put" was usually referred to as General Putnam only in official reports. That's the kind of rough old fighter he was. He met Nat and Shad in an upstairs room of Hollis Hall at Harvard College. He was in dirty work clothes, shirtsleeves and all. Rumor was that when he had heard what had happened at Lexington and Concord he had stopped work on a stone wall he was raising, jumped his horse, and ridden a hundred miles in eighteen hours to reach Cambridge at sunrise. He was nearly sixty years old, and he was built like a sturdy keg: short, stocky, as tough as wooden staves.

Knowlton introduced Nat and Shad along with a quick résumé of their history, and Old Put put a grin on his pumpkin face and rose to give their hands a good pumping.

"That was some fight, boys. Wish I could've been there. Good ride, too," he added, jerking a nod at Nat. "I met Billy Dawes this morning. Warren sent him into Boston."

He paused and glanced down at a paper on the table before him. "We just got the butcher's bill for yesterday's fight here. Some fella with a mathematical turn of mind figured it all out. I reckon you boys would like to hear the results."

"I reckon we would, General," Shad said.

"The British," Put read from the paper, "suffered seventy-three killed, one hundred seventy-four wounded, and twenty-six missing. Total of two hundred seventy-three casualties. We had forty-nine killed, forty-one wounded, and five missing. Total of ninety-five casualties."

Nat was staggered by the small number of British casualties. Old Put nodded dourly. "This mathematical fella figured that our boys fired no less than *seventy-five thousand* shots at the enemy. In other words, only *one* bullet out of every three hundred found its mark." He turned to Shad.

"Don't seem possible, does it?"

Shad shrugged, saying: "Anything seems possible, General, when you're trying to fight a war with a pack of clod-footed farmers."

"Yes—farmers." Putnam looked at Shad and Nat. "And actors and Indian scouts. Interesting army we're building here." Suddenly he addressed himself to Shad in what Nat thought was pure gibberish.

"He'onwe Hadi'nonge ne ha'sennowa'nen?"

"Waa'gen he'onwe Odinon'sot ne Nangannia'go," Shad promptly replied.

Knowlton dropped his mouth. "What in heaven's name sort of heathen talk is that?"

Old Put chuckled softly. "That was Seneca, Captain. I asked him where all the chiefs had gone, and he told me to hide in the place where the beavers build their lodges." His eyes swung to Nat.

"You boys mind hooking up with our outfit until Warren

returns? We desperately need a veteran like Holly. I could make him a training sergeant and you his corporal."

"I'd admire that, sir," Nat said. "Though the only thing I know about war is what I saw yesterday along the Concord-Lexington road."

"That's all right," Knowlton said, smiling. "The only thing you need to teach discipline to farmboy recruits is a strong build. You seem to have that."

"Yes, sir," Nat agreed. "But I don't think I'll have to use it."

"I take it you don't know much about Connecticut farmboys, Corporal," Old Put said dryly. Nat grinned.

"No, sir. But I guess you don't know much about Shad Holly."

Sergeant Holly was all business when it came to whipping green farmboys into something that resembled soldiers. Right off the bat at cockcrow he had Corporal Towne turn them out of the Harvard barracks. Some of the young fellows were tardy about rolling out of their bunks, and some even wanted to give Nat a bad time, and—when Nat merely shook them by the shoulders to rouse them—Sergeant Holly nearly had a fit.

"Corporal Towne! What in holy Hector's name you think you're doin'? Waking your palsied grammaw? That ain't no way to get a sleepy recruit onto the parade ground!"

And he gave Corporal Towne an object lesson—grabbing a cot in one ham-sized fist and raising it up and swinging it over and on top of the groggily shouting recruit.

"*That's* how you get a recruit up!" he announced.

Corporal Towne had no trouble rousing the rest of the sleepyheads.

Sergeant Holly marched his gang of "greenies" away

from the bad influence of New Hampshire and Massachusetts onlookers, driving them into a clearing in the woods. Then he had them fall in and stand at attention while he delivered a bombastic speech about war.

Towering, immense, sweating like a Greek slave, he swaggered up and down in front of the stiffened, half-frightened ranks, roaring like a walleyed, goaded bull.

"You green hicks think war is romantical, do you? You think it's pretty uniforms and swords and roses and *bee*-utiful girls wavin' lilac-scented hankies at you, eh? You think it's a tidy officer dyin' *see*-renely in the arms of his *bee*-reaved staff pals with flags wavin' over his powder-wigged head and angels flap-a-doddlin' in the background, I suppose?

"Well, take it from me it *ain't no such a thing!* It's *you* with a doggone muskit ball in your gut, and you on your hands and knees alone in pig weed with your head down and tryin' to suck air into your busted lungs! *That's* war! Dirty, bloody, muddy, screamin' sufferin' war! No drums, no fifes, no flags or lacy hankies. Just you and a bullet where it don't belong! And why? Well, I'll tell you why.

" *'CAUSE YOU DIDN'T LISTEN TO YOUR SER-GEANT WHEN HE TRIED TO TELL YOU HOW TO TAKE CARE OF YOUR SIMPLE-MINDED SELVES, THAT'S WHY!*

" 'Cause you're all as green as grass! 'Cause you don't even know which end a the muskit a ball comes out of! 'Cause you think a cartouche box is some kind a French bin for storin' stock fodder! By blim-blam-blankity blazes would you just look at them slab-faced, cow-milkin', clod-footed hicks I'm supposed to lick the redcoats with!"

(This appeal was addressed to Corporal Towne, who was

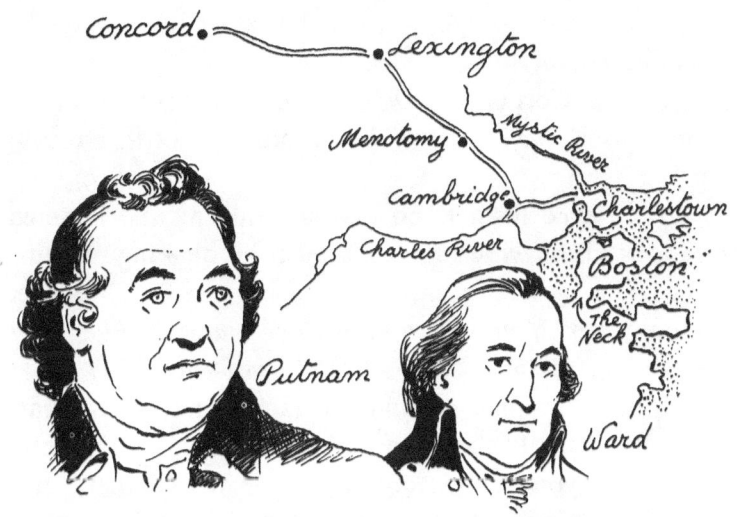

standing embarrassedly to one side—and who had no reply to make.)

Shad suddenly seemed to take on the tall, broad aspect of a two-storied brick building as he leaped forward and loomed threateningly over a young, white-faced little farmboy.

"*YOU!* How old are you?"

"Sssssss-six-six-sixteen, sss-ir."

"Don't call me 'Sir'! I'm Sergeant Holly! Got that? After you been in a battle—and if you somehow live through it— you can call me 'Shad'! Sixteen, eh? So. How many men you killed so far?"

"Nnnn-none, sir, I mean Sergeant Holly!"

"*NONE!*" Shad pawed at his face and snatched his British officer's hat from his head and threw it into the dirt and took a kick at it.

"By the time I was sixteen I'd kilt five Mingos and two

Delaware sachems and one Catawaba subchief! And this here greenie that's supposed to soldier aside of *me* says he ain't killed *nobody*!"

(Again to Corporal Towne—who had never seen an Indian himself, save for two Tuscarora squaws in Norfolk once.)

Shad retrieved his hat and gave it a dusting and jammed it on top of his burly head. He glared at his quaking recruits.

"Now! I'm gonna let you boys in on a secret. Men get killed in a war! You want a know *how many* men get kilt? I'll show you. Detail—atten-*CHUN!* Eyes—*RIGHT!*"

Their heads snapped around and each man was now staring fixedly at the back of the neck of the man on his right.

"The man you're now *lookin'* at," Shad told them in a grim voice, "*ain't* comin' back alive from this here war!"

At first you could see a sort of sympathetic compassion in their young eyes as they thought: *Say, this poor fella I'm lookin' at is as good as dead right now.* Then a sort of slow dawning of fear crept into their eyes, and one or two of the quicker ones turned their heads around to the left—to find the man standing beside them staring at *them!* You could almost hear them thinking it: *Wait a minute here—that blame fool's starin' at ME!*

Shad slapped his thigh and let out a whoop of laughter.

"By gobs! Just lookit there at their faces! *Haw-haw-haw!* You ever see a funnier sight, Nat? Lookit them scared-green faces!"

The recruits, as they began to catch on, started to grin sheepishly. Yessir, that Sergeant Holly was some fella—for a Pennsylvanian! They reckoned they were right proud to be under the charge of the biggest, toughest, fightin'est soldier in the American army.

8

SOUNDS LIKE HOT TIMES, EH NAT-O?

Early in May Nat and Shad were ordered to report to Putnam's quarters. They found Major General Warren waiting for them.

"Good to see you again, Shad. Understand you're making a little army of your own."

"I could make a better one, Doc, if me'n' Nat here had some powder'n' ball to teach these boys something about guns. I ask you, how can an army train, let alone *fight*, without ammunition?"

"That's the big problem," Warren admitted. "Powder. And it's the same in every province in the country. We have plenty of men but not much to arm them with. We now have nearly fifteen thousand troops camped right here— against Gage's five thousand in Boston. Yet if Gage knew how poorly equipped we were. . . . " He shrugged, then smiled his quiet smile.

"What I need is more information. Jessie Greene is still in Boston, and Billy Dawes is working with him. I'm sending you two men into Boston. You'll be Billy's contact.

Figure out some plausible reason why the two of you should have to go in and out of Boston. Make it good! Gage has his Tory spies everywhere, and they suspect everyone—even themselves."

Nat pulled Pitcairn's pistols from his belt. He had been forced to carry them around like a pirate because the thievery that went on in the American army was scandalous. It seemed to be a game: which provincial regiment could steal the most from the next provincial regiment. Shad claimed that the Rhode Islanders were the absolute worst—that they even put *him* to shame; and by grab that was going some!

"General, would you take care of these for me?" He pushed the pistols across the table to Old Put. "I took 'em off Major Pitcairn's horse at Lexington."

Putnam hefted the weapons with a belligerent look on his salty old face. "Lobsterback guns, eh? Maybe we can give 'em back to the major someday—through the muzzle end!"

The plan was Nat's. He sprinkled his clothes with dust, hung out his shirttail, stuck a few wisps of straw here and there on his jacket, and then tied a rope about his waist and handed Shad the free end, leashing himself with about a ten-foot lead. His lower jaw dropped, his brows drooped, the spark of intelligence faded from his eyes, his shoulders slumped, his arms dangled purposelessly. He said: *"Daaah."*

The perfect picture of the village idiot!

Shad tied the end of Nat's leash to a tree and left him there for a few minutes while he went to "find" a few things they would need. Shortly some of Gridley's artillerymen came by and paused to laugh at the simple Simon who said *"Daaah"* at them and flapped his arms and finally picked a daisy and started eating the petals. The artillerymen went away roaring, and Nat felt satisfied that he was convincing in the part he was playing.

Shad returned bearing a wicker basket loaded with vegetables, and they went on their way, Shad leading Nat along by the rope.

They had no trouble crossing the American barricade on the Neck, but the British fortification on the Boston end proved to be a horse of a different color. A pompous, bewigged captain sat behind a field desk with a bad case of high blood pressure. His grinning men prodded the genial Shad and the idiot Nat over to the desk with their bayonets.

"Yes! Yes! Name. Occupation. Residence. Business in Boston?" the captain snapped, reaching for his quill and inkpot.

"Wash Georgington, Major sir," Shad replied promptly. "I'm a farmer, I am, and I live over to Cobble Hill, I do, and I'm takin' my Uncle Oscar to see his Aunt May. That's on my mother's aunt's side, that is."

The captain put down his pen. He blinked at Shad. Then he blinked at Nat, who was gawping at him witlessly and letting saliva drool out of his mouth.

"*Your* Uncle Oscar? *Him?* You're *his* nephew? Gad's my life, man! You're twice his age!"

"Yessir, Colonel. My mother's ma, Grammaw Gert, didn't have him til late, and her half sister, Aunt May, is——"

The captain ran a hand up under his wig. "Grandmother Gert, Aunt May, your mother's. . . . Deuced take it! This doesn't make sense at all! Never mind! Never mind! Let the bumpkin speak for himself. Why do you keep him on that rope?"

"To keep him outa trouble, General."

"Trouble? Trouble? What trouble does he get into? What's wrong with him?"

Shad tapped his right temple significantly. "Mule kicked him in the head when he was a tad. He ain't overly bright. But he does so love to visit his Aunt May. He's takin' her some greens, he is."

The captain's blood pressure was soaring. He'd never heard of such nonsense! Plague take the Americans for a pack of dolts.

"You! You!" he pointed at Nat. "Confound it! Stop gawking over there like an idiot! Come here! *Here! HERE!*" Nat immediately started to straggle off the other way. He stopped short at the end of his rope and flapped his hands.

"Oh, my *word!*" the captain cried. "Pull him in on the rope, cawn't you?" he shouted at Shad. "Do *something* with him!"

Shad started reeling Nat into the desk, cooing at him kindly.

"Now, Uncle Oscar. Be a good boy. Come see the nice officer."

Uncle Oscar didn't want to be a good boy. He wanted to make a mess of things with the captain's inkpot. And he did: picking it up and spilling it all over the captain's carefully printed reports and down the front of the captain's jacket and into the captain's lap.

"*Gad's my life!* What has the idiot *done!*" The captain's blood pressure took off through the top of his wig. "Cawn't you restrain him, you great fat fool of an oaf! Look what he's done!"

"Now, Uncle Oscar, that was a bad bad boy!" Shad

chided his naughty "uncle." "Aunt May is gonna be put out when I tell her what you went and done to the nice man. Now—what've you got to say for yourself?"

"Daaah," was what Uncle Oscar had to say for himself.

"Out! Out! Get them out of here!" the captain literally screamed.

Shad took off down Orange Street, dragging his giggling "uncle" after him like a tin can on a cord.

Billy Dawes was his usual unperturbed self. But Jessie Greene was frankly worried.

"You'd better not come to the warehouse again," he told Nat and Shad. "Now that my place is closed and I'm out of business, it might look suspicious if you were noticed too often. After this, arrange to meet Billy or Harvey Allen at the corner of Queen and Tremont."

"What's wrong, Jessie? You think you're watched?" Shad asked.

Jessie nodded distractedly. "That's what I feel. Possible I'm wrong—but Gage's Tory spy system is like an octopus. It's everywhere."

"Gage's got a real shrewd fella in charge of his intelligence service," Billy said. "Nobody knows who he is, *except* Gage. He's just called Mr. X. We can't seem to get a line on him."

Billy had considerable news for Nat and Shad to take back to Warren and the committee—some good, but most bad. Gage's Irish recruits were half-heartedly thinking about deserting the King's army and joining the rebels; Admiral Graves, in command of the King's ships in the harbor, hated General Gage's guts because Gage had taken all the marines away from him to use as footsoldiers. So be it; Graves wouldn't do a thing to help Gage in any way if he could get around it. That was the good news.

"The bad," Billy said casually, "is that six regiments, the Thirty-fifth, Forty-ninth, Sixty-third, Sixty-fourth, Sixty-fifth, and Sixty-seventh, are due to land in Boston next week. This will push Gage's rank and file up to maybe seven thousand. Also Colonel Timothy Ruggles is forming four regiments of Tories: the Loyal Legion, the Loyal Americans, the Loyal Fencibles, and the Loyal Loyals, or something like that. They seem partial toward green. You'll know 'em by that color—if they ever get around to uniforms.

"And—in about two weeks the frigate *Cerberus* is due. She's bringing General William Howe, General Henry Clinton, and General Johnny Burgoyne. The popular feeling here in Boston is that with such capable officers as these, the British will shortly put our slouchy, unruly citizen army to rout; chase us all back home and keep us there."

He winked at Nat. "Sounds like hot times, eh, Nat-o?"

Nat and Shad made two trips across the Neck that week to visit "Aunt May." Both times they met Billy at the corner of Queen and Tremont, but he didn't have much news for them. The following week it was Harvey Allen who slouched up to them as they loafed around the corner.

Allen couldn't help grinning in his beard when he saw Nat looking like a dog on a leash. "Want a bone, fido?" he asked.

"Your head will do for a start," Shad growled. "What news? Where's Billy?"

"Just come from 'im, I did. 'E's down to the docks waiting to see the British ships come in. Sent me on to find you;

says we've got some Tory trouble the Boston Committee wants you to look into. Shad, you're to go up to Lynn. There's a rumor some Tories 'ave 'oled up in a swamp there and mean to try and form a regiment. If it's true—gather up all the patriotic lads you can lay 'ands on and take the bleedin' Tories prisoner." He turned to Nat.

"There's a Tory stronghold atween Athol and Petersham, Towne. But we got a report that a patriot 'ad a secret powder depository in 'is cellar afore 'e cleared out. The Committee wants the report affirmed afore it decides to act on it. That's your job, bucko. Get in there, see if the perishin' depository exists or not, and report back."

"By grab, the Committee don't want much, does it?" Shad cried. "They're sendin' Nat right into a nest a Tories *alone!*"

"Well, I know it, don't I!" Allen retorted. "But Billy says the Committee picked 'im because 'e's the best man for the job. 'E's a giddy actor, ain't 'e? Well, they want 'im to *act* like a Tory. Billy says it'll be a breeze for Towne."

"Billy says! Well, tell Billy them Tories will breeze holes through Nat if they catch him on their ground!"

"Never mind, Shad," Nat cut in. "I can handle it all right." In fact he wanted to do it. He was growing almighty tired of playing Uncle Oscar the village idiot. After all the excitement he had experienced on April 19, he now found that he was becoming restless with inactivity.

"There's the lad!" Allen said. "The 'ouse you want is two miles south of the Athol-Greenfield road. It's the Peter Lark 'ouse. Remember that: the Peter Lark 'ouse."

Nat nodded. "I won't forget. Peter Lark." Then Shad took him by the shoulders and held him firm.

"Natty, you take care. Hear? By grummit, if anything

was to happen to you, I'd feel that *I* was to blame. After all, I got you into this here war!"

"No, Shad. That's not right. You didn't get me into it any more than Doctor Warren got you into it. It's something that had to happen, and it just seems to have happened in our time. I guess we were born for it, all of us."

"Just the same," Shad growled. "If you get yourself kilt, I want to met the fella that done it! And when I do I'm gonna fix him like I seen a Mingo fix a lobsterback once. I'm gonna skin him bald! And I ain't talkin' about no wig neither!"

9

THEY HANGED THEM
BY THEIR HALTERS

In the woods, under the cover of the pinnate leaves, Nat lifted his head toward the splotchy sun and heard, as from far off, the lonely *pak* of a musket firing in the wilderness.

Hunter, he decided, hopefully.

He spoke the word in his mind, then shoved it into a dark shelf with all the other mute words—not forgotten, but idle until he needed them again. In the past four days he had acquired the habit of speaking to himself soundlessly, holding intense conversations, firing questions, snapping answers. It was good practice, in case he was apprehended by Tories.

It also helped his nerve. It was like having a friend who was as apprehensive, as uncertain as he was. Which was an asset, because it gave him strength to calm this invisible ally. For instance, he could say: *Nat, you slughead, don't get spooky because you heard a gun. We've already decided that it's a fella hunting.*

Hunting what?

Rabbits, you idiot!

Beyond the forest a meadow lay empty, and by now the echo of the musket's cough was long gone. Out in the field the sun was heavy, yellow, and there was nothing more. Only early summer sights and sounds: a breeze, warm and thick in the weeds, and the hum of bees.

Go on. It's safe.

He stood up and slapped dust from his hips. He looked at his clothes, at the baggy, nondescript pants, the faded jacket with its tarnished, shilling-sized brass buttons; and he wondered if the American fighting man would always look like a tattered tramp.

Now that he was definitely in Loyalist territory, he had become exceedingly wary. The first thing he did was remove his hat and shove a green cockade in it. He stepped into the meadow, not liking the arrangement that confronted him. He knew he should skirt open ground, but now he had no choice. To the east was a bald hill. He couldn't use that. And westward the meadow sprawled indefinitely. Might take hours to follow it on around. To the north—just a hundred open yards from where he stood—the woods picked up again.

Get going, Nat-o.

He hurried into the meadow, his right hand touching the brassbound reassurance of one of the major's pistol butts in his belt. The grass fell without effort under his brogans, flattened, bobbing back to half-mast in his wake, quivering. He wondered if someday soon armies would be marching across this peaceful meadow, leaving trampled havoc behind. He sincerely hoped not. He hoped that the issue might be resolved at Boston. But he doubted it.

Keep your mind on what you're doing! Watch those trees!

He smeared dust that turned muddy across his brow with the back of his damp hand. *All right. I'm watching them. All right I——*

Something moved in the shadow of the woods—brown carrying blue.

Nat grimaced. Caught in the open with fifty yards still to go. He dropped into the grass and snatched for one of the pistols.

The wall of the forest opened like a small green door in a vast green room, and a bay horse picked its way into the meadow, head swinging down to nuzzle the rippling grass as it moved. The rider was wearing a blue militia coat, red facings and all!

It simply didn't make sense. How could a Yankee soldier ride openly through Loyalist territory without being blasted from his saddle?

The rider was coming closer, closer, his head hanging negligibly on his chest, just as if he didn't have a thing in the world to worry about. And then it made sense. The man in the militia coat was on the same business Nat was on— only he was a spy for the other side.

Nat's finger curled about the trigger. He didn't like the range. Too far for a fellow who still didn't know enough about pistols. He glanced right and left, frowning. He'd have to make a stand. No time to retreat. The thing that was in his favor was that the Tory spy wouldn't know that he, Nat, was an American scout.

He came to his hands and knees. Then he started to raise the pistol, slowly. The rider lifted his head and his eyes drifted on to Nat.

Nat couldn't believe it. In a tense magical moment that suspended time he recognized Ralston Morbes. And in that

same moment Ralston recognized him and knew what he was doing there, and both of them knew that the other could not go on.

Nat fired at the blue coat, the pistol jerking *ka-blam!* in his hand.

The horse's head went up, nostrils flared, eyes back-rolling, its mouth a band of white against a blob of red. Ralston rose with the rearing nag, his hand snatching frantically for his saddle holster. Then he had his pistol out, and he seesawed the horse's head down, crouched forward, booted home his spurs, and came on.

Missed! Missed by a mile!

Nat dropped his empty pistol and grabbed for the other one as he rose from the grass to stand spread-legged before the charge. He swung the pistol up and squeezed the trigger.

Cock! Cock it, you fool!

His thumb jerked back the hammer with a *clik-clok*, and he aimed at the blur of blue chest that loomed above him. The gun roared.

Through the whirl of blue smoke he saw Ralston start to tip over, dropping his pistol as the horse veered sharply right, and for a moment he thought horse and rider would separate. But they didn't. Ralston, crumpled in the saddle, clung on somehow, as the panic-stricken horse turned down-meadow and went plowing through the saffron weed. Ralston was clutching his right arm.

Nat lowered his pistol, thinking: *I must reload*. But he didn't. He listened to the soft thudding of the runaway horse, watching Ralston ride away from him. It had been a rotten, sorry incident, and its repercussions might prove disastrous for Nat. But at least Ralston wouldn't be doing any spying for a while.

He picked up his other pistol, thinking: *Jerked the*

trigger. Shad would have a fit if he knew that. He turned away heavily, feeling the full pall of his weariness and the sharp taste of bitter regret in his mouth.

The shade of the woods was a welcome relief, but his thirst was powerful. The ancient, lightning-scarred trees seemed unnaturally large and gnarled as he approached the old grove-circled stone house he believed was his objective. The thickets that abounded the area were as dense as witch-hobbles, while underfoot fat mounds and rocks in the weedy, pitted earth looked like skulls swelled to gigantic proportions.

Nat started for the house, treading cautiously. He was watching, not listening, when a voice spoke suddenly on his right side.

"Hold up, bub."

Nat jerked to a standstill. He looked right, forcing himself to keep his hands at his sides. *Don't try for a pistol,* he warned himself. *There's one aimed at you right now. Relax . . . you're a Tory.*

A thick, close-to-the-ground man twice Nat's age was watching him from behind a sumac. He held a horse pistol in his hand, pointed casually in Nat's direction. He was dressed in a filthy, green-dyed buckskin jacket that bore linen sergeant chevrons on one side. His face was like his clothes—darkened by exposure, ragged with whisker-sprouts. His skin looked unhealthy under its varnish of sweat and tan.

A real abysmal brute, Nat thought, sizing the man up. Better go easy with him.

He smiled, raising one hand to touch the green cockade in his hat.

"Hello, brother. Do you have water?"

The Tory's eyes were like gimlet holes in a pan of shining dough, sly with suspicion. "Who are you?" he asked.

"Scout for General Gage out of Boston," Nat said indifferently. He held out his hand for the canteen he saw on the sergeant's hip. The horse pistol followed his movement.

"What regiment?"

"Loyal Americans. Can I have a drink?"

"What were you going to that house for?"

"To find water, I hoped. Fella I met down the road said it was empty. Said it belonged to a dad-gasted rebel."

"What fella?" the sergeant wanted to know.

Nat flashed angrily. "What's wrong with you? Can't you see who I am? How do I know what fella? Some farmer, that's all!"

The sergeant grinned, showing an appalling set of disordered and stained teeth, and holstered his pistol.

"Awright, bub. You know how it is these days. A body can't take no chance . . . and you was comin' from the wrong direction."

Nat nodded and uncorked the offered canteen. He knew how it was. Two days ago he had come upon two men who had died not very valiantly. Some militiamen had told him that the two men had been Tory spies. The spies had been hanged by their own halter straps. He drank.

He relaxed then, handed the canteen back, and sat on a rock.

"Quiet here," he commented, reaching for a weed stalk to chew. "Not like Boston. Always mob trouble." He noticed that the sergeant was still watching him with the same sly expression.

"How are things here?" he asked. "Are the Loyalists going to make a countermovement?"

The sergeant pinched some tobacco shards from his pocket with thumb and forefinger and threw them into the back of his mouth. He gave them an explorative chewing, then said:

"I wouldn't know. They don't confide in me much. I'm just a common citizen soldier—like you."

Nat glanced at him. The man grinned and squatted on his heels in the dirt before him. He spat expertly at a droning bee and canted his eyes back to Nat.

"Kind a risky to come through rebel lines with that cockade, ain't it?"

Nat matched the man's casual air. "I only put it in my hat a little while ago, so you fellas wouldn't shoot me for a Reb."

"Ain't you kind of young for this work?"

"Ain't you kind of old to be asking so many questions?" Nat countered. The sergeant laughed and flapped a hand disarmingly.

"I just like to know what's going on. Who's your corps commander?"

"Ruggles, Timothy Ruggles."

"Yeah? Ain't never heard a him. What's he look like?"

"Oh, he's thin, fortyish, straight dark hair. Good-looking man." Nat made up an imaginary man. What was wrong with this Tory? What was he fishing for? Nat threw his chewed weed away. Time to be moving, to get away from this man and his endless questions. He would have to swing back to the stone house later and take a look at that cellar.

"Well, I'd better be on my way." He leaned forward to stand up.

The sergeant's hands flashed at Nat's stomach, and for a moment Nat thought the man was offering him a hand up;

but instantly—and even that was too late—he knew he was wrong. The sergeant straightened up, grinning. He held both of Nat's pistols, held them pointed at Nat's stomach.

"Best lift them hands of yours a trifle, Reb, so's I can see 'em better. Not real high—don't want to strain yourself."

Nat felt a vacuum form from his stomach to the back of his throat.

"What's wrong with you?" he cried.

The sergeant wagged one of the pistol barrels under Nat's nose. His little porcine eyes were mean with a savage kind of ecstasy.

"You stepped in the wrong hole, Reb. Ruggles ain't about to be fortyish. He was born in seventeen eleven. I *thought* you were the man I wanted from the time I first laid eyes on you comin' up the hill. Now you just open your——"

A sudden hubbub rang out to the east of them, and a sharp voice called: "Dance! Dance, you over there?"

The sergeant bit at his lower lip and looked vexed. He took a step back from Nat and made a motion with one of the pistols.

"Awright. Go on. Move out. You and me got friends to see."

Nat turned into the woods. He looked at the grassy path running off into the blue shadows. He saw a golden shaft of dust-swirled light where the sun knifed through the upper terraces like a benediction.

They hanged them by their halters, he thought. *And I don't even have a horse.*

A group of armed Loyalists—fourteen or fifteen in green-dyed butternut—sat in and by a rutted road, smoking, chewing, talking about the war. To Nat they looked like a bunch of dispossessed scarecrows clumped together in common misery.

I'm a bluebird, Scarecrows, he thought. *Turn me loose and scare me away.*

One of them, a wild-eyed man with a snow-white beard, looked up and sang out: "Looky there at ol' Dance! Reckon he's gonna shoot him all the tall fellas he can find so's to make hisself out as the tallest Tory in town?"

Other bearded, sickish, fierce-eyed faces tilted up to survey Nat. Some laughed, but they were a hungry, tired crew, and their laugh lacked humor. They had lost their humor after Lexington and Concord, and they were never again to recapture it. The rest only looked and made no sign.

Sergeant Dance pushed Nat into their group and left him standing with his hands up, surrounded by a ring of faces that bore the weathered aspect of townsmen who weren't used to extensive outdoor living.

"You boys stop your bullyraggin'," Dance growled authoritatively. "This fella is a rebel spy. I caught him in the woods trying to sneak into Peter Lark's old house. I figure——"

"You didn't *catch* me sneaking anywhere!" Nat cried. "You just up and jumped me without warning. Why don't you tell the tru——"

Dance's face bunched in anger, and he swung the right-hand pistol barrel at Nat's head. Nat side-stepped, bringing down his hands, but something hard and positive jabbed into his back and a voice said in his ear: "Best stand still, bub. With your hands up."

Nat raised his hands again, and turned to face Dance.

"I'm not a spy. I told you I was a scout for Gage. That's why I was coming from Boston, to find out——"

"I *know* why you was coming!" Dance cried, and saliva from his mouth flaked the air. "Now I'm gonna show you other boys something!" He jammed a pistol point into Nat's stomach. "Open your shirt!"

"What?"

"You heard me, Reb. Open your shirt! Show these boys what you're wearing around your neck."

Bewilderedly Nat opened his shirt. For a long, empty moment Dance stared blankly at Nat's bare chest. Then a tall, rather dignified-looking man spoke up.

"What exactly did you expect to find on the boy, Dance?"

"A roll of birchbark, that's what! He must a hid it somewhere else on hisself. C'mon, you fellas! Bear a hand and we'll strip him!"

Birchbark! The word rang through Nat like a Cassandra call. How in the name of all that was sacred did Dance know about the Abenaki message? He put up no struggle as the band of Tories turned him and his clothes inside out. He was too stunned even to speak.

"Looks as though you picked on the wrong man, Dance. He's clean."

"I tell you he's the *right* man!" Dance insisted.

"Well how would you know whether he was carrying birchbark or not?"

"Because it's my business to know! Because I'd been informed that a tall, husky young fella would be coming along to try and get into Peter Lark's house. And I was supposed to waylay him."

A trap, Nat thought bleakly. *I was deliberately sent into a trap under orders.* But why? And who did it? Allen? Dawes? No, he couldn't believe it of Billy, even though Harvey Allen had said that Billy had passed him the order.

Allen . . . Shad had said that Allen was a deserter from the King's navy. But had Allen really deserted? Or——

"He fits the description, don't he?" Dance was still insisting. "Even if he don't have the message on him. And he was tryin' to get into Peter Lark's house. A rebel's house! I tell you he's a spy!"

Nat knew what was wrong with Dance. The issue had become a personal thing with him. He was the kind of man who had to be right, always. He couldn't admit to mistakes —no matter who paid for them. He was the embodiment of the underprivileged bully, hating authority, culture, intellect, hating anything he couldn't understand. But were they *all* like that? The tall one there, with the gaunt, thoughtful face; he looked like a decent sort. *Appeal to him,* Nat thought.

"Look here," he said. "I don't know anything about birchbark messages. I was sent up here from Boston because General Gage needs to know what sort of Loyalist support he can count on from outside."

"Oh, that's a pretty story, that is!" Dance snarled. "But it won't wash. You told me you was in Tim Ruggles' Loyalist corps; yet you think Ruggles is only forty years old—when every man here knows he'll never see sixty again! And in case you didn't know, Reb, Ruggles ain't got straight dark hair. He's as *bald* as a coot!"

It looks bad, Nat thought desperately. *It is bad. I've got to convince the rest of them that I'm not the person Dance knows I am.*

Again he turned to the tall dignified soldier, who was standing beneath a twisted oak (and even the tree hampered Nat's thoughts; he had to force his eyes from it, away from the naked, sturdy limb that jutted over the dirt road like a gallows crossbeam).

"I didn't say I *knew* Ruggles. He's the corps commander. I've only seen him from a distance. I'm in the Loyal Americans' Company."

"Who's your CO?" someone asked.

"Philips."

"What's his first name?" someone else asked.

"I don't know. He's just Captain Philips."

The tall man shoved away from the tree. He approached Nat with an intense look. "What's *your* name?"

"Harry Lang." Nat's eyes flicked past the man's head. He saw the waiting oak limb. The drumhead court had begun.

10

HE WISHED HE COULD HAVE
SAID THANKS

It was like a game, Nat thought. A game he had played as a boy.

Who am I?

Do you have ears? Yes.

Are they long? Yes.

Are you a donkey? No.

(Who's the CO of the Loyal Fencibles? Uh—Captain Thorne.)

Are they floppy? Yes.

Are you an elephant? No.

(What's Lord Rawdon's military rank? Col—no, uh—major.)

But the game ended too soon . . . .

The president of the court got up from the berm alongside the road.

"You gave too many wrong answers, Reb. This court has decided that Dance is right. You're a spy—and there's only one thing we can do with spies. All right. Get it over with."

Hands caught Nat's arms, pulled them down; more hands

at the small of his back, lashing his wrists; grunted breath breathed in his left ear; a man jarred shoulders with him, muttering: "Sorry." Now a horse was being led from the shelter of a sugarbush, a bareback nag. Dance was grinning.

They lifted Nat high, his legs forking the horse's back. He and the horse were going to take a ride—a very short one. Right then Nat almost went to pieces. He couldn't face what he knew was coming.

"Don't do it, you fools!" he shouted. "You haven't given me a fair trial! Where are your officers? I have the right to be heard by——"

"Calm yourself, bub," a voice advised. "Take it like a man."

I can be a man, Nat thought wildly. *But I don't want to take it! Not like this. Not from a blame rope!*

A youth mounted on another sorry nag came up behind him and fitted a noose over his head. The rope's end was knotted to the limb above Nat's head. He looked up. That limb was a living extension of that living tree. And in a moment that tree would bear dead fruit. Nat pulled his head down and looked at the tall man with the thoughtful eyes. That was all—just looked at him.

The tall Loyalist contracted his mouth and stepped into the center of the road. "Hold on, Dance. It seems to me that *your* men constituted that whole court. You didn't let the rest of us have much say."

He turned to a silent group sitting slightly apart on the off side of the road.

"What do you men think? I don't feel that this boy had a fair trial. He wasn't heard by any of our officers. I think someone should take him back to our headquarters in the swamp and turn him over to Major Wells."

Nat realized then that these men were from two different Loyalist companies, and there was obviously ill feeling between them. Dance blew his cork. The tall man started to shout. Then they all came together in a clump. They argued, curses shattered above their heads, they stamped, pushed, a knifeblade glinted, hands reached, they hesitated, pacified, argued again.

Nat waited, watching from his perch, his head canted in the noose.

What if this horse decides to wander off while they argue? he wondered. *Or what if that boy waiting behind me decides to take matters in his own hand and takes a cut at the horse's rump with that switch he's holding?* He swallowed—tried to, anyhow.

The tall man turned abruptly from the group in the road and walked toward the tree. Nat stopped breathing. He watched the Tory coming—watched him with such intensity that he didn't even understand what the man said to him at first.

"What?"

"I said you aren't going to be hanged now. We're sending you back to our major. You'll be held as a prisoner of war until it's proved that you're either a Loyalist or a rebel. I wish I could send some of my fellows back with you, but we're on patrol now. Those rebel militia up at Athol are giving us a bushel of trouble."

Nat let out his breath. Then he looked at Dance. The sergeant was standing apart, spitting tobacco juice angrily at the ground. He roused himself and slouched over to a slim, rag-and-tatter corporal and began to talk to him quietly. The corporal, a shifty-eyed youth with a saber stuck in his belt, glanced at Nat and smirked, nodding.

The tall Tory called to the corporal. "Neb—you going to take him?"

"Sure," the youth muttered, and he went for his horse.

The horseman behind Nat loosened the knot about his neck and lifted the noose clear. Nat worked his head between his shoulders, then looked back at the empty noose dangling from the limb.

A blow from Neb's saber was better than that, he decided. Much better.

They rode off together—the Tory with the mission Dance had given him and Nat with his head full of desperate plans. They'd relashed his hands in front of his body, enabling him to hold the reins. He kept on the off side of Neb's horse, so that Neb would have to cut across with his saber instead of down . . . when the right time came for Nat to make his break.

The road ribboned out before them, long and straight, with the unfenced fields sloping down on either side and sumacs squatting in clumpy clearings where the fences had been before the coming of the Tories and their cookfires. Ahead of them a forest humped into the sky like a green mountain and the road tunneled in like a dark hole.

It'll happen in there, Nat thought tightly. *Neb will finish me the way Dance ordered him to.*

He closed his eyes for a moment, trying to think out what he should do, how he could beat Neb to the punch. It wasn't going to be easy: aside from the saber, Neb also had a pistol in his saddle holster.

"Halt, fella!" Neb suddenly called, "—till I tighten my girth. Saddle's slippin'."

Nat didn't believe it. Neb was only using it as an excuse to throw him off guard.

The woods hovered over them, bathing them in cool green shadow. Nat sucked his breath. This was the moment —the last moment. Neb was dismounting, his left foot still in the stirrup, his right leg swinging over the horse's rump. For a second his back was turned. Nat gritted and lashed out with his foot, catching Neb between the shoulders. The Tory's head snapped, his arms flying out at crazy angles from his body.

"*YAH!*" Nat bellowed at his horse's head, and he buried his heels into the nag's flanks. The horse spurted from a dead halt, cannon-shot into the shadowy grove. Nat clutched frantically at the reins as the horse seemed to scoot right out from under him, his lashed wrists hindering his control and his grip. He felt a sick sensation in his stomach.

You're going to fall! Hang on, draggit all! Hang on!

A thin spindly branch hung down over the road. The wild horse veered from it sharply, and Nat's hard-pressed legs slipped along the naked flanks, the sick sensation materializing into a cold stone of positive conviction. He was going over.

All at once he was free of the horse, turning in the air, hearing the muted beat of the hoofs going away, seeing the tilted green weeds leap at his face. He threw up his lashed hands and—*whamp!*

The earth and trees clashed together, and the sky, all splotchy black and turquoise, fired in his eyes, and he rolled and gasped for his breath and couldn't seem to get it past a constriction high in his chest. Then he came to his knees.

Far back along the lonely road Neb was aiming the horse pistol at him. Nat heard the *zzzunnn* of the ball carry past his head, saw a little globe of pearly smoke break out of Neb's fist, and then he heard the appalling crash of the shot.

Nat struggled to his feet and ran for a laurel tangle. Would Neb remount and follow him? He paused inside the thicket, listening to the tattoo of hoofs on the road. They were drawing away. But he knew what that meant. Neb would go after Dance and the others. They would try to cut him off from the east. Dance would see to that.

Where was he? East was that way? Yes, it was. Good. If he could reach the meadow where he had fought Ralston, he might be able to escape. The terrain beyond the meadow, he recalled, was a perfect wilderness; mounted men would find it impossible to ride through.

But he had to get there first, and he was only on foot while Dance's patrol would be coming on horse. Eight (maybe more) sturdy horses against one tired soldier. Eight angry men against one scared scout.

Run, Nat-o! The hounds are out!

He ran. He went with fear crouching and gibbering on his shoulders. His feet chopped at the turf and he wobbled dangerously. His lashed wrists forced him to keep his arms bent out in front, and this awkward position played havoc with his equilibrium.

In the woods, through the reaching, tearing thickets, he thrashed, stumbled, fell, and came up with an alacrity that went beyond age or strength, that was born of pure fear. And he ran ran ran. He ran all the way to a shack in a disordered clearing that stood a scant two hundred yards west of the meadow he was seeking.

And then he heard the distant beat of the hoofs.

He paused, gasping, and leaned against a tree to regain his sight and sense of balance. *Can't make it,* he said. *They're too close and I'm played out. Scarecrows, you've got me. My wings are clipped.*

He looked at the shack—a knockdown shebang affair,

lost in age and neglect—and at an old woman who stumped heavily on the porch to dispose of a pan of greasy water. He watched the water plop on the ground, saw it fan out into a curved silver shield and fall again, dappling the gray-brown earth a rich black. He started walking.

The old woman watched him, stared at his lashed wrists, and reached for a ratty broom that leaned upright against the siding. Then a girl came through the doorway and over to the woman's side. Nat stopped in the dooryard and looked up at her. She was the type of girl he particularly liked—quietly pretty. She watched him with wide gray eyes.

"I need help," he told them hoarsely. "They're after me, close behind." He held out his hands. "I don't have a chance like this."

The woman stared at him for an immeasurable moment with a face so worn-out it looked like a mournful statue face from some long lost city.

"You're a rebel," she said in a low voice.

Nat shrugged. He didn't actually think of himself as a rebel.

Her hand moved away from the broom, letting it stand awkwardly by itself for a moment, then it toppled to the porch with a hollow clatter. The hand went toward her scrawny neck and she lifted her head. They could all hear the pound of the hoofs in the thicket.

The girl jerked at the woman's elbow. "We've got to help him, Grandma. He's helpless." But the old woman did nothing, said nothing. She listened to the horses coming.

Nat shook his head resignedly and turned for the trees.

"Wait!" the girl called. "Don't run. Under the house, quick. Up under the porch steps."

Nat grinned at her impulsively and dropping to his knees

began to squirm between the foundation opening. A square shadow pool stretched before him, rippled by the clods of dirt and the dark nameless objects of discarded refuse. He crouched and scurried into the dank angle where the under-carriage of the steps met the ground, and a razorback pig went scooting out of there all asqueal with fear.

Nat felt sweat bubble over his face and down his neck like a spring welling out of the earth, and heard—close now —the *clop-cloppity-clop* of the hoofs. Through the cracks in the slats he watched the fast blur of tufted fetlocks. Bits of dirt and stone spattered against the boards. He closed his eyes and lowered his head. *Go away, Dance.*

" 'Day, ma'm. You see a fella afoot come this way?"

"Yes. He came along right smart a few minutes ago."

"Head for the meadow, did he? He's a rebel spy, ma'm."

Go on, Dance, Nat prayed. *Chase off into the woods after me.*

"No, he didn't. He's right here—hiding under the house."

The words were just words at first. Nat heard them, accepted them, shoved them back in his mind . . . then snatched them out again. But they were different the second time; they were distorted with disbelief.

"Grandma! *No!*" the girl cried.

"Fan out! Jump, will you? Neb! Get around back, quick!"

Where could he run to? What could he do? If he could only stand up . . . if his hands were only free. But he re-laxed, not even fighting them when they dragged him from beneath the steps and shoved him up to the grinning Dance. He noted that there were only five of them now.

He looked at the parchment face of the old woman.

"The rebel militia burned our home in Athol," she told

him, tiredly. "Because we're Tories. Drove us out into the night with nowhere to go."

Nat nodded. He'd heard stories like that before—from both sides. He didn't know why he had expected her help. A civil war was always the worse kind of war. It seemed to intensify the hate. But the girl, he saw, was genuinely sorry for her grandmother's action.

Dance tapped Nat's chest with a pistol barrel.

"Gave us a little run, eh, Reb?" he sneered.

Neb pushed through the Tories, his thin face dark and mean, saying, "He give *me* more'n a little run——" He struck Nat's chin with his fist.

Nat lurched backward, his sight blurred by blue and green. Hands grabbed him again, shoved him to his feet, held him. A voice raged in his ear.

"That'll be enough of *that*, Neb Harker! We're holding this boy's arms. Or maybe you didn't notice? You want to fight him so blame bad, I'll cut his hands loose and let him go at you!"

Nat turned to that man. If he had ever thought of himself as an actor in his life, he was going to have to prove it now.

"Mister, listen to me. I don't know what Dance has against me, or who he's mistaken me for; but I can prove I'm not a rebel, because I killed a militiaman half an hour before I met Dance. Now if I were a rebel, I wouldn't go around shooting the men on my own side, would I?"

The man didn't seem to know what to think of that. He looked at Dance, but not for advice. His eyes were angry. He was getting sick and tired of this whole business. He didn't believe in hanging folks, anyhow—Rebs, Tories, or otherwise.

"How?" he demanded. "How can you prove it?"

Nat pulled his arms free and gestured toward the meadow.

"Out there. The rebel's body is out there."

"He's lying in his teeth!" Dance cried. "For cripe's sake, you ain't gonna listen to him, are you?"

The girl shoved her grandmother aside and came to the head of the porchsteps. "The least you can do is let him show you," she said to them. "That's not much, is it?"

The man who didn't approve of hangings thought about it. He looked toward the meadow, then at Nat, then at Dance.

"I've got to know for sure," he said finally. "If we swung him, and then found out he was telling the truth—I couldn't face myself when I tried to shave in a mirror. What do you other fellas say?"

They seemed to be in accord with him. But Dance wasn't.

"Are you out of your minds?" he raged at them. "He's tryin' to stall, hoping something will turn up. What's wrong with you blind idiots? I tell you this is the fella I was supposed to catch!"

"You've *got* to go look!" the girl insisted. "You have to give him that much of a chance. And, Grandma, you shut up! Do you want to see them hang him right here in the dooryard?"

The man who opposed Dance nodded grimly. "Come on, you, march," he barked at Nat.

Nat looked back at the shanty as he started away with the five Tories. The old woman had gone back into the house, but the girl was still on the porch watching him out of a blond mist of hair. All he could do was look at her. He wished he could have said "Thanks."

The important thing was that they didn't retie his hands behind his back. If they did, it was all over for him. Deliberately, he intwined his fingers and held his arms stiffly in front, making himself look as awkward and helpless as possible. Dance walked at his side, a pistol in the small of Nat's back.

They waded deep into the meadow, the sun warm and heavy on their backs. Nat led them to the spot where Ralston's nag had trampled the weeds. He stopped and lowered his head, feigning repugnance.

"It was the first man I ever killed," he said huskily. "I don't want to see the body."

Neb and the other three waded a little further on, looking right and left. One of them called back, "Well—where is he?"

"A bit to your right," Nat said. "See where that depression is?"

Dance moved one-two steps forward, squinting at his companions.

"Well, is he there? Eh? He ain't, is he? I told you it was a blame lie. You ain't about to find no body out there."

Nat's eyes were searching frantically through the weed. He'd stopped at the approximate spot where he thought he remembered seeing Ralston drop his dueling pistol. Then he saw it—six feet away. He glanced at Dance. The Tory's back was half toward him.

Now or never, he said.

He took two big oblique steps, swept up the pistol in both hands, and pointed it at Dance. Everyone seemed suspended by shock as they watched him cock the hammer.

"It's up to you fellas," he called. "Any of you can shoot me—but I'll blow daylight through Dance first. If you want him to live, then pull out of here."

The hesitation ticked off ten more seconds; then Neb whined.

"What'll we do, Sergeant?"

"Shoot him!" Dance cried, but there was something wrong with his voice, his eyes too. Nat grinned mirthlessly.

"You're still holding my pistol, Dance. Why don't *you* try to turn and shoot me—if you're so willing to die?"

But Dance didn't want to try that at all. He didn't know what to do. His eyes were wild with indecision.

"Well, somebody do something!" he implored the Tories.

The man who had stood up for Nat back at the shack shrugged finally, saying: "Guess we better get out of here, boys."

"No! Wait!" Dance wailed. "Don't leave me! He'll kill me!"

"Yes, and he'll kill you if we don't go," the same man said. He didn't really seem to like Dance much.

"Mister," Nat said to him, "I'm sorry I had to trick you like this, but it was the only way I could think of to save my neck."

"Guess we can't blame you for that, son," the man said. "Do the same thing myself, if I was in your spot."

"Well, I want you to know that I'm not a spy. I was sent here to see if there's a powder depository in the Lark house. That's all."

"Shucks, old Peter Lark didn't have a pound of gunpowder to his name. We went through his place from cellar to attic after we ran him off. Looks like somebody gave you a wrong steer."

"Looks like it," Nat agreed.

The four men drifted slowly across the meadow, looking back from time to time. Nat stepped up to within two feet of Dance, aiming the dueling pistol at the Tory's stomach.

"Now drop my gun . . . now ease the other one out of your belt and drop it . . . now take out your knife and cut my wrists loose . . . easy! Don't get rambunctious. Mind where I've got the pistol pointed."

Dance minded. He cut Nat loose as gently as if he were a nurse handling a week-old baby.

"Now drop the knife, turn around and head for the woods. We're going to have a talk, you and I."

Nat returned one of Major Pitcairn's pistols to his belt, kept the other in his hand, and threw the dueling pistol away. So many guns made him feel like Blackbeard the pirate. He marched Dance into the east woods and made him stand in front of a tree, while he seated himself comfortably on a flat rock nearby.

"Now—talk. How did you know I was coming to the Lark house?"

"I got nothing to say," Dance replied surlily.

Nat pulled the hammer back on the pistol. It went *clik-clok* distinctly. Dance's eyes started to flutter nervously. He wet his lips.

"Here's how I see it, Dance. You're a Tory spy, and it's my duty as a patriotic American to uh—eliminate you. Unless . . . "

Dance watched the pistol rise slowly to aim, his eyes growing wider and wider.

"Wait! Wait, I'll tell you! Honest. But I don't know much. I've been in the pay of Gage's central intelligence for a year now. All I do is go to Boston once a month and receive my orders."

"From who?"

"I don't know from who. I never see his face. We always meet on the docks at night, and he's always muffled up. Nobody knows who he is. He's just called Mr. X."

Mr. X again. "Come on, Dance," Nat demanded. "You must know *some*thing about the man. Think!"

Dance eyed the unwavering barrel of Nat's pistol distractedly.

"Well, but it's dark, I tell you! And he keeps hisself covered. I can't tell nothin' about him—except—except that he stutters sometimes."

"Stutters?"

"Yeah, when he gets excited he stutters a little on his aitches."

"His what?"

"His aitches. Like h-how, h-have, h-here."

I I

IT'S NOW OR NEVER, BOYS!

When Nat returned to Boston Harbor he found that the situation between the British and the Americans was still at a stalemate. The city was blockaded by land, but as long as the King's fleet kept open communication with the sea, Boston was not properly besieged. The Americans had no siege guns to batter the city into submission and not enough trained soldiers to attempt a storming attack. And the British had seemingly learned their lesson at Concord and Lexington; they weren't about to try another outside offensive.

Nat made his way to Cambridge and to Hollis Hall at Harvard. Right off the bat he blundered into Shad Holly in the lower corridor.

"Natty! My goodness, boy, where you been? I've had fellas lookin' ever'where for you!"

"Shad, I've got to see General Warren. That powder depository at the Lark house was a trap. A Tory spy knew I was coming and was waiting for me. I had to tell eighty-two lies to keep my neck from being stretched by hemp."

"A trap!" Shad yelled. "I should a knowed it. Should a knowed just as soon as I reached Lynn and couldn't find no

136

more Tories than you can find snow flakes in July! I spent three days beatin' around in them gafocky salt marshes with a bunch of milishy lookin' for Tories that didn't exist!"

Nat nodded. "Whoever sent me to the Lark house wanted to be certain I went alone. So they sent you on another wild goose chase."

"What'd they want you for, anyhow?"

"That Mr. X who is running Gage's central intelligence wants that roll of birchbark from the Abenakis. Look, Shad —I don't like to think it, but everything adds up to a mighty strong possibility that someone in the Boston Committee of Safety is a Tory spy. You better come with me to see Warren."

"You can't see him, Nat. He ain't here. And anyhow, Old Put is sendin' me on a detail to Hog Island out in the bay. The other day Gage sent four sloops and thirty men to Grape Island to gather up hay for his horses and some beef cattle for his troops. Old Put is beatin' hisself over the head with a cane he's in such an uproar about it. He wants me to take my recruits over to Hog and Noddle Islands and round up all the grazing livestock there afore Gage hooks them too.

"You better come along with me, Natty, so's I can keep an eye on you. We'll worry about this Abenaki business later. Tell you what. I've heard that that fat old lobsterback Admiral Graves has landed a batch of naval stores on Noddle Island. Won't he turn hopping mad if we was to find 'em and snitch 'em right out from under his red nose? By juckies, that man's just as greedy as a skinny pig at the trough. He might even decide to fight us, that's how greedy *he* is!"

Shad led his small detachment through Winnismet and on around to Chelsea. By wading a narrow shallow channel they reached Hog Island and went to work driving off all the sheep, cattle, and horses. The livestock secured on the mainland, Shad collected his men and led them, wading again, over to Noddle's.

The recruits had rounded up about three hundred head of livestock when the lookout gave a shout from a bald hill.

"Sergeant Holly! Sergeant Holly! Them Britishers is sendin' a warship agin us! She's comin' hull-down like a bat out a hades!"

Shad grinned like a fat boy at a surprise birthday party.

"All right, boy!" he called back. "Don't come all apart like an old woman with the palsy. I seen lobsterbacks afore! C'mon, Nat. Let's you'n' me get up on that hill and see what old Granmaw Graves is up to. You other boys—herd them stock on back to the mainland!"

From the crown of the hill Shad and Nat and the lookout stood in the salt grass and watched the armed schooner *Diana* tack toward the island. Shad chuckled throatily.

"Didn't I tell you old Greedy Graves would kick up a ruckus when he seen us makin' off with his goodies? Looky there. Bet he's got him fifty marines aboard that li'l' old tub-a-war!"

As the *Diana* approached the shallows handily, she dropped her fore and main sails and glided slowly up-channel on her outer jib and staysail. The reduced speed was enough for the British to lower a flotilla of small-boats loaded with marines, yet still retain her headway.

"Let's go," Shad snapped. "There's gonna be a fight. Ain't *nobody* takin' them cows from me without somebody in a red coat pays for it!"

Before Nat and Shad could reach the bottom of the hill, the *Diana* opened fire on the recruits fording the channel between the two islands, as they drove the livestock across.

"That's it!" Shad raged. "You stupid lobsterbacked pea-wits! Blow up perfectly good cows so can't nobody use 'em!"

Which was exactly all the damage the *Diana's* guns were doing—inflicting casualties on the livestock; the Americans remained untouched. But it was messy in the shallows, with shells plowing up great cascades of white water, and horses stampeding, and cattle going down and thrashing up a chaotic bedlam, and the sheep *baa*-ing in panic.

Shad and Nat regrouped their men on Hog Island, letting the livestock look out for itself. Nat found an irrigation ditch in the marsh, and Shad strung his recruits along it and told them to crouch down and open fire on the marines who were now pressing after them.

The muskets went *pak! pak! pak!* along the ditch, and the marines hesitated, then started to bear to the right. Shad shoved his burly head forward and glowered at the beach.

"Aw, for gravy's sake!" he howled. "Where are all the dead men? What are you fellas shootin' at—seagulls? Didn't I teach you hickheads how to shoot? Didn't I? Now lower your aim and let me see you hit something besides clouds!"

Then the marines sent a volley and all of the recruits threw themselves everywhichway in the bottom of the ditch. Shad stood up and snatched off his officer's hat and started mangling it between his mighty hands as though he were wringing out a wet shirt.

"Oh my *ga-wd!* What have I just seen? Will somebody tell me that? What have I just seen the empty-headed, pea-witted, manure-pitchin' rubes I've been bustin' my back to

train into soldiers *DO?* Here! Git offn your blame bellies!
You ain't Daddy's little farmer boys no more—you're
fightin' soldiers of the *You*-nited Colonies! What're you
afeerd of? Them lobsterbacks ain't never *hit* nobody. They
been tryin' to hit French'n' Injuns for a hunnerd years and
ain't none of 'em made the grade yet! They can't shoot no
better'n you do!"

He jammed his hat back on his head and snatched for a
musket.

"*HI-YI!*" he roared. "Who wants it?" And he raised the
musket and it kicked *Pa-Lam!* in his hands on the up-swing.

Probably none of the marines wanted it, but a corporal
caught it—swinging half around, dropping his musket, and
sinking to one knee in the salt grass.

"C'mon!" Nat yelled. "Fire! Fire, for grab's sake! You
want Sergeant Holly to fight 'em by himself?"

The white-faced recruits came to their knees and leveled
their weapons over the berm. The fight was on.

It was brisk and lively, and the musket balls whined
through the weeds like bees. Outnumbered, the Americans
held their position in the ditch doggedly, and the marines
pulled back. The farmboys unanimously decided it was a
great Yankee victory.

"Hurrah!" they shouted, tossing their hats. "Hurrah for
Sergeant Holly!"

Sergeant Holly didn't say "Hurrah." He said: "Aw, shut
up and follow me." He led his detachment down to the
fringe of the marsh to reconnoiter the enemy.

The enemy was in trouble. The *Diana* had come into
conflict with an adverse wind and now the tide was against
her. She couldn't get out of the box her zealous captain had
sailed her into. "Granmaw" Graves was coming to her aid.

Like a mama hen leading a line of chicks, Graves—in the armed sloop *Britannia*—was bringing twelve barges from the fleet to tow the *Diana* off.

"Hi, boys!" someone yelled. "It's Old Put! Lookit him come!"

The doughty old Indian fighter, his hat gone, his shirt-sleeves rolled up over his chubby arms, was herding 1,000 foot soldiers and two fieldpieces across Chelsea Neck. Nat could hear them singing a version of Yankee Doodle that had become popular since the Concord-Lexington fight.

> Father and I went down to camp,
> Along with Captain Gooding,
> And there we see the men and boys,
> As thick as hasty pudding.

> Shot the redcoats in the road,
> Whipped 'em neat and handy!
> Going back to whip some more!
> Yankee Doodle Dandy!

"C'mon, boys," Shad ordered. "Let's get back to the mainland and join Put. We ain't gonna see no more fightin' out here!"

By the time the barges had secured their tow lines to the *Diana*, Putnam had his cannons in position and his infantry hunkered along the shore. In order for the barges to work the *Diana* out of the box, they were going to have to warp her around in a wide arc, bringing her within firing range of the American position.

Nat glanced at the setting sun as he trotted down the beach in Shad's flat-footed wake. In another few minutes

twilight was going to make accuracy in aiming mighty poor.

"Hi, Holly!" Old Put yelled. "Get your men along that hummock there! Open fire as soon as they come into range. Don't let them twelve-pounders of theirs scare you. There ain't no more harm to 'em than a bowling ball!"

" 'Less you go to stop one with your head! Which I don't aim to do!" Shad retorted. "By grab, Natty, I reckon Old

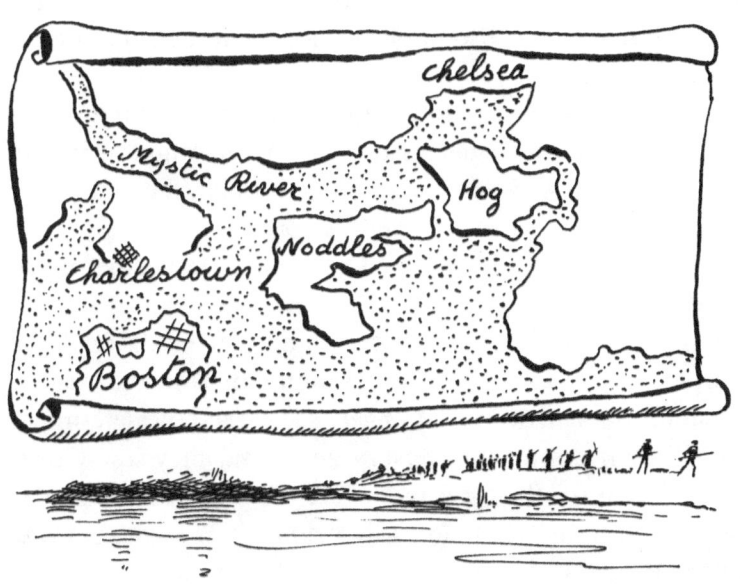

Put aims to take that there schooner. Leastwise, he's sure setting about to try!"

As the *Diana* drifted down upon the shore where Putnam's provincials waited, the British twelve-pounders opened up with a jarring, air-slamming *KA-BLOWM! LOWM!* and great shocks of orange flame winked over the darkening water. All along the shoreline you could hear the militia officers yelling: "Fire! Fire! Fire!"

Putnam's two fieldpieces belched like flame-mouthed dragons and kicked backward out of their own smoke, and the musketry went *plam-plam-plamming* like an endless series of doors slamming.

"Hi! Yi! There goes her fore topgallant!"

The *Diana's* fore topgallant mast leaned at a crazy angle as overstretched stays started to snap loose, making little popping noises like distant pistol shots. The armed schooner began to lose way.

"It's now or never, boys!" Old Put was bellowing from the beach. "Follow me!" He went at the water in a fat-waddling trot and started wading through the wine-dark shallows, holding a sword over his head.

"*Heee-yuu-ahh!* Let's go! Let's go! Everybody in the water!"

Again it was happening—the thing Nat had seen Jonas Parker do at Lexington and the militiamen in the road at Menotomy; men so full of anger, so adamantly determined to pull their powerful adversary down that they stood up to face certain death. Now they were wading out to meet it, not giving a hoot as long as they could come within closer range to get just one good crack at "Granmaw" Graves' lobsterbacks.

He was in the water now with the major's pistols in his

hands, and men were sloshing around him on all sides. The dusk was deep and the *Diana* and the barges stood out only as faint silhouettes. All the cannons had ceased fire, but the *pak-pak-pak!* of the muskets went on and on, making little quick jabbing fingers of light from the water and from the rail of the schooner.

The dim half-figure of a militiaman, waist-deep in the water, moved in front of Nat, holding his musket over his head. Suddenly he lurched backwards, dropping his gun with a splash, and said: *"Aauh!"*

Nat watched the man swing around in the water, grab at his shoulder, and almost go under. He started wading toward him, calling:

"Hold on, mister! I'll get you!"

The water went *toomp! toomp!* around him as musket balls spat in, and he put both pistols in one hand and reached for the wounded man with the other, getting him around the back and under the armpit, and then started backing out, dragging the poor devil half under in his stumbling haste.

A short stocky recruit bumped into them on the dark beach. He was wringing wet and nearly in tears.

"I was nearly out to her, Corporal! I was gonna try and board her like I knew Sergeant Holly would want me to and then I stepped into a blame hole and went under and soaked my powder and my priming and——"

"All right, Tim. All right. You did fine, just fine. Help me get this fella up to the high ground. Mind his shoulder."

Far out across the troubled water he heard Shad's ear-quaking *HI-YI!* and then a multitude of disembodied voices yelling: "They've cut her loose! They're a-leavin' her, lads!"

It was true. The British were helpless in the dark. The

towing barges had cut loose and were rowing away. The *Britannia* had come ghosting in to cover the *Diana*, and now she was taking off the schooner's crew with her boats. Fascinated by the spectacle of a dying ship, the Americans ceased fire and simply stood in the water watching the black hulk of the *Diana* drift hopelessly aground.

She struck with a loud, spine-tingling grind and heeled sharply over on her starboard beam and came to rest like a huge beached whale. Old Put's dream had come true—he had taken the *Diana*.

Nat waded across the shallows again and swarmed aboard the wreck with a couple hundred other Americans. It was like stepping into a lively little scene from a production of Dante's Inferno—with the ragamuffin militiamen slipping and stumbling and cursing along the canted deck, all the rigging and lines hanging limp and crazy, and an outbreak of bull's-eye lanterns throwing cone-shaped splashes of fiery light wildly about.

Officers were cursing out their orders in sharp, Yankee-nasal tones, and most of the men were paying no attention to them at all—everyone doing what he felt like doing and helping himself to what he wanted or thought he could cart away or could talk two or three other fellows into helping him cart away; and so it took nearly all night for the disorganized troops to remove four four-pounders and twelve swivel guns and salvage the *Diana's* ironwork and stores.

The schooner had been set afire, and the first coldly bright glints of dawn were breaking out of the east when Nat, wading ashore with a smoldering firebrand, came upon Jessie Greene sitting on an old half-buried timber beam. Jessie, soaking wet and nursing two blistered hands, looked up with a quick smile.

"Why, Nat! I didn't know you were along on this."

"Jessie! What're you doing here?"

"I was chased out of Boston, Nat. Just as I'd feared—a British patrol descended upon my winery yesterday. I barely escaped out the side alley with some important papers. I think they caught Ed Norton."

"What about Billy and Harvey Allen?"

Jessie shook his head. "I've no idea where any of the fellows are. Perhaps they're all captured by now."

"I think someone blabbed, Jessie. Someone on the Committee is a Tory. Which reminds me—whose brainstorm was it to send me to Athol to look for the powder depository in Peter Lark's house?"

Jessie looked bewildered. "Athol? You mean you were ordered into a Loyalist stronghold? Who gave you the order?"

"Allen. He said Billy had passed it on to him."

Jessie's face tightened. "I don't understand it. But I can assure you, Nat, the Committee knew nothing about it. Yes, I believe you're right: someone talked. If I'd waited a moment longer, I'd be in Stone Jail right now."

"How did you end up way over here?"

Jessie smiled mildly. "Warren was gone when I reached Cambridge, and Putnam was just leaving to march against the *Diana*. So I thought I'd tag along. This is the first crack I've taken at the British."

Nat looked at Jessie's blistered hands.

"You don't even have a weapon, do you?"

"No. No chance to find one. I merely came along as a volunteer." He glanced at the pistols in Nat's belt. "I see you're armed . . . I wonder if you'd do me a favor, Nat? I've been asked to remain behind with a platoon of men to watch over the *Diana* until she burns down to the water.

General Putnam fears the British may return and attempt to save the ship. But——" he smiled rather helplessly, "my guardsmen seem to be scattered far and wide already. I can't find a single one of them. Are all of the militia so slipshod about the performance of their duty?"

Nat grinned and took a seat on the timber. "I'm afraid so. They're a pretty independent bunch. You either like 'em or you can lump 'em. They don't seem to care much which you choose."

Jessie looked at the scarlet-orange banners of flame whipping up from the crackling wreck, and said, "Well, independent or not—they kept Graves from recovering the *Diana*. Putnam's a grand fighter."

"Speaking of grand fighters—have you seen Shad Holly anywhere?"

Jessie chuckled dryly. "No, but I believe Shad was close by—from the sound of those war whoops."

The last of the stragglers had taken themselves and their bundles of loot off across the marsh, and dawn was now spreading the land. Nat and Jessie watched the *Diana*'s standing and running rigging go up like a dry hay fire. Showers of glowing sparks crackled in the chill air and fizzed in the water about the canted schooner. Even if the British did return they would find precious little to salvage.

Jessie turned to Nat with a smile and drew a silver flask from his pocket. "Calls for a celebration drink. I discovered this flask of Madeira in the captain's cabin while going through the ship's papers this morning. Also——" He dug into his other pocket and produced a set of small gold-plated cups designed to fit one inside the other like little flowerpots.

"We'll drink a toast to Putnam and the *Diana*."

Nat would have preferred something to eat. But he was in favor of the toast. Jessie set two of the little cups on the timber between them, filled them nearly to the brim, then passed one to Nat.

"H-here," he said. "H-here's yours."

I2

THE OLD SPYMASTER STILL
HAS A FEW TRICKS
UP HIS SLEEVE

Nat stared at Jessie Greene.

"What was that?"

"Your drink. Take it."

Nat took the cup and looked at it. Then he looked up. Jessie had his cup to his mouth, but he wasn't drinking. He was watching Nat over the brim, waiting. The hand holding the cup had a slight tremor.

"You said 'H-here's yours,' " Nat told him.

Jessie stared at him. "Did I?"

"Yes . . . " Nat looked at his cup again. He held it to his nose and sniffed the lemon-colored liquid. He didn't know enough about Madeira or any other wine to tell from the odor. Very carefully he lowered the cup and set it on the timber. Jessie hadn't moved as much as a muscle. He was still staring at Nat, his cup poised before his mouth.

"You're not drinking yours," Nat said.

"I'm waiting for you."

"Jessie—do something for me. Say: he hoped to hear her howl."

Jessie's eyes were as opaque as two paving stones. He said, tensely: "What's wrong with you, Nat?"

"You tried to knife me the night you killed the messenger from the Abenakis. You set up the trap for me at Lark's house, and you duped Billy into passing the order on. Your Tory name is Mr. X."

"I don't know what you're talking about. H-have you lost your mind?"

Nat glanced at Jessie's cup. "Drink your Madeira, Jessie."

Jessie didn't drink it. The tremor in his hand became more pronounced. He wet his lips, his tongue feeling for them hesitantly. Nat drew one of his pistols and aimed it at Jessie's chest.

"Drink it."

Jessie looked at the cup he was holding. Then he shook his head slightly and lowered the cup to his lap. He gave a heavy sigh.

"The Madeira wasn't from the *Diana*'s cabin, was it?" Nat prompted him. "You brought it with you from your warehouse, hoping for a chance like this—to get me off alone."

"It isn't poison, Nat. Believe me. Only a strong sleeping drug."

"I don't believe you. Once I knew you were Mr. X, you couldn't afford to let me live."

"Listen to me, Nat. I want to explain something to you about war. Uh—first—would you mind lowering that weapon a bit? I don't like pistols without triggerguards. They're much too touchy."

Nat lowered the pistol. Jessie was a small man; he could bust him like lamp glass if he had to. "You don't have to tell me about war. I've been fighting one—while you've been hiding in Boston knifing your friends in the back."

"They aren't my friends!" Jessie flared. "I'm a Tory. Always h-have been. No Whig rebel is my friend. I'm loyal to the King, and I do his work in the best manner I know. You and your illiterate rabble are trying to take this land away from the King and the rest of us loyal Englishmen. And it's my job to try and stop you!"

"Nice job," Nat said acidly. "Knifing an unarmed and probably unsuspecting man in a black alley."

Now that he was excited, Jessie's faltering aspirates were becoming more noticeable.

"I h-had to do it! I h-had to get rid of him before h-he could reach the Committee with that birchbark message. H-he showed up at my warehouse alone and told me what h-he was carrying. I knew h-he h-had to be taken care of right away, but I couldn't do anything there because Norton was in the rear of the warehouse. I told h-him I'd take h-him to Warren. Once I got h-him in that alley I did what I h-had to do. Then you showed up before I could find the birchbark."

"What's so important about the birchbark?"

"I've already told all of you what it said."

"No. You told us only enough so that we wouldn't want the message to go on. I think it said something else, otherwise—as a Tory—you wouldn't have had any reason to stop the messenger."

Jessie made an angry gesture with the hand that held his cup of drugged wine. "I'm telling you the truth! The message said———"

All at once his arm shot up and out, and the liquid contents of the cup splattered blindingly into Nat's face and eyes. His hand reflexed on the pistol as he lurched sightlessly backwards.

Pal-lowm! And he knew that shot was a total loss, as he shoved to his feet pawing at his eyes with his left hand. Then, blurrily, he could see again—could see Jessie standing ten feet away, grinning at him with Major Pitcairn's other pistol in his hand. The loaded pistol.

"The old spymaster still h-has a few tricks up his sleeve, eh, Master Towne?" Jessie taunted him. "But you were right about the Madeira . . . I *can't* let you live." He glanced down at the pistol.

"But first—throw over that roll of birchbark."

Nat shook his head. "Your pal Dance couldn't find it on me; and you won't have any better luck."

"Where is it?" Jessie snapped, and Nat almost grinned.

"You'll never guess."

"You're lying," Jessie decided. His thumb *clik-cloked* the hammer.

Something moving beyond the stern of the wrecked *Diana* caught Nat's eye—a British patrol boat rowing slowly around the stern of the ship, estimating the extent of the damage. A squad of redcoated marines sat amidships with their musket butts grounded on the floorboards.

At his side, Nat let his empty pistol drop to the sand. Then he raised his hands above his head and let out a yell.

"Help! Help me! He's a rebel spy!"

The marines—unexpectantly coming upon two men standing on the deserted beach, one with a pistol in his hand—were thunderstruck by Nat's cry. So was Jessie. His head snapped toward the patrolboat.

"Lookout! He's armed!" Nat yelled.

Jessie started to swing back to Nat, raising the pistol as he turned. "What are you trying to——"

Five or six marines threw up their Tower muskets and fired on general principles. Nat felt one of the wild bullets tear through his jacket, going away. But it didn't consciously register in his brain. He was watching Jessie Greene.

Jessie's torso twisted on his legs, paused as though suspended in a remarkable state of imperfect balance, as he tried to raise his head, tried to raise the pistol; then he swung to the left and kept right on going, pitching into a headlong crumple in the damp sand.

Nat waved to the marines. "Hold your fire! I'll be right out!"

He picked up his empty pistol, then stepped over to Jessie's body and got that pistol too. With an elaborate, businesslike stride he turned and started for a sand hummock beyond the old timber beam.

"Nah then! Nah then!" an impatient voice called from the boat. "What are you about there?"

Nat, not slackening his stride, held up a hand for patience.

"He has some papers here in the weeds!" he shouted. "Be with you in a minute!" And he went up the hummock and down the backside and out of view of the patrolboat, and kept right on going into the marsh.

The young actor still had a few tricks up his sleeve, too, eh, Master Greene?

Dusk had settled its heavy benediction over the harbor as Nat emerged from the salt grass and returned to the shore. He had spent the long lonely day in the marsh waiting for the twilight. Now it was time to go to work. After a half-mile search along the shore he found what he'd been hoping to find: one of the small-boats the British had lost from the *Diana* the day before.

There was only one oar left in the craft, but that didn't perturb him greatly. The distance that separated Noddle's Island from Boston was under half a mile, and if the ebb tide was right, the current should bring him down on the city somewhere around the North Battery.

To be sure, he was going to have to be gosh-awful careful, because by the terms of Gage's Port Act it was unlawful for any *vessel* whatsoever to load or receive any *cargo* whatsoever in any *place* whatsoever in the entire Massachusetts Bay. Gage had been known to construe his order to the extent that a dinghy was a "vessel," a person was a "cargo," and any island, creek, wharf, sandbank, or rock was a "place." Anyone attempting to violate the Port Act in any way was instantly subject to capture by the King's eagle-eyed fleet.

Once he was in midchannel, Nat discovered that the tide, as in the affairs of men, was turning contrary. There was a definite drag to the northeast, for which he had no use at all, and it proved to be a Herculean task to keep headway on the little boat with only the one oar, and keep her bow to the North Battery.

The city glittered and gleamed under her miniature aurora borealis of night lights, and—sometimes standing amidships, more often on his knees, stroking right, stroking left—he gradually drew down on her. Once he had worked his way into the slack water and knew he was all right, he changed his course to land between Hudson's Point and the Copp's Hill Battery. The shortest and safest line of retreat he could think of was to cross between Hudson's Point and Charlestown and make his way to Cambridge across the Neck.

But that was for later. First he had to get the roll of birchbark.

He stroked the boat into a quiet shadow pool of water and under a deserted dock. The weeds were high in that place, and the off-chance of any casual passer-by observing the boat was slim. He landed and struck out for Sudsbury Street.

He thought he would feel at home in Boston, but he didn't. The city had become a Tory stronghold—a malignant canker on America's hide. He stayed with the inside streets, with the shadows and alleys, and he reached Jessie's warehouse without incident. He gave the secret knock on the door, then, as he waited, eased one of the pistols from his belt. He really had no idea whether Ed Norton could be trusted or not.

Norton's eye studied him through the peekhole. Then the door swung open and Nat stepped in and felt for Ed in the dark with his left hand, found him, and planted the pistol barrel in Ed's flat stomach.

"You're probably as right as rain, Ed," he said. "But I can't take any chances. Jessie tried to kill me this morning. He was a Tory spy in Gage's pay."

Ed seemingly couldn't believe the startling news. "Bb-but you can't *mean* it, Towne! You can't! Not Jessie. Not Jessie Greene!"

"Yes, I mean Jessie. He's the Mr. X Billy was talking about. I mean—he *was* the Mr. X. I killed him."

It was too abrupt, too much for Ed to consume in one quick gulp.

"Towne! You ain't serious! You can't mean you *kilt* Jessie!"

"I did the next best thing," Nat admitted. "I had him killed by his own side. Now listen. I don't have all night to play question and answer with you. There's something I've got to pick up and get out of Boston with. If you're on the level, then you'll find some way of finding the rest of the boys. Tell 'em to get the heck and gone out of Boston. There's no telling how much Jessie has spilled to Gage."

"It must have been quite a bit," Ed said after a moment's deliberation. "General Howe has stated that he'd give five hundred men to take Doctor Warren; and Gage has issued a proclamation of martial law for Massachusetts which calls us an 'infatuated multitude—conducted by *certain well known* incendiaries and traitors.' "

"Lead the way to the basement steps," Nat ordered. "I've got that Abenaki roll of birchbark hidden there."

"In the stairwell?"

"That's right. Funny, isn't it? The night I made the ride with Billy I was afraid something might happen to me; so as I followed Billy up the stairs, I shoved the birchbark under one of the casks of wine Jessie kept stored there . . . under a cask of Madeira."

With the roll of birchbark around his neck again, and with a hasty farewell handshake from Norton, Nat started back toward Copp's Hill and his boat. He might have made it too—to the boat, into the channel, to Charlestown, and so on to Cambridge—except for the cat.

The cat was fat and it was inclined, in its overfed condition, to be slow. It was after the rats that lived under the wharf (more out of natural habit than hunger), and it knew that the best time for rat-catching was at low tide. So it was there—hunched and tubby, with the tip of its tail a-wag—in the shadows of the dock, when Nat slipped through the high weed and started for his boat.

Just then a slim rat broke cover and the fat cat pounced and the rat took three quick leaps—left, right, and gone, and the fat cat slid to a stop on the mudbank and looked everywhere at once in baffled bewilderment, and then let out a loud *mee-ouwr* of frustration.

And it was just at that moment that a patrol of Loyal Americans was passing along the street end of the wharf, and the sergeant glanced downward to see what it was that had bugged the cat—and saw Nat slipping through the shadows.

"Halt! You there! Halt, or we'll open fire!"

Nat looked up and saw the moon beaming on the barrels of six muskets, and (remembering what had happened to Jessie Greene in a similar situation) he halted.

"Come up out of that! Let's see what yer about at this time of night. Another giddy rebel making for the mainland, I'll be bound!"

"And what's so wrong with that?" Nat replied, coming forward, and picking up the sergeant's trend of thought. "If a man's no Tory and is sick of living with a city full of Tories, who's to stop him?"

"Well, there's no crime in that," the sergeant admitted. "But let's have a look at yez first. Come up into the light."

It's all right, Nat told himself. *You've got them half convinced already. Don't panic. You're just another patriot making for the mainland.*

He climbed up the bank and took a belligerent stand in the moonlight as the patrol surrounded him. "Sure, it's a foine thing," he cried in the Irish brogue he'd adopted from the sergeant, "whin a man can't even go whir he wants in this blessed country!"

"Now calm yersilf, bucko," the sergeant said. "All we're after is a few civil answers to a few civil questions."

"A darlin' arrangement it tis! A darlin' arrangement!" cried Nat. "Ask away, me foine bhoy!"

"It's yer name I'll want first."

"Sure, 'tis Michael Flynn, same's it's always been!"

" 'Tis yer address I'm after next."

"Sudsbury Street, as anyone who knows Michael Flynn can tell ye!"

"And yer after jining the bloody rebels, is it?"

"Jine the rebels yer backside! Who said sich a thing? Sure, I'll fight the man that siz sich a lie! To the mainland, I'm off! To get away from the whole giddy pack of yez— rebels and Loyalists alike!"

"Say now, lad, you seem to have a bit of the Kerry in yer tone. Tis there I'm from mesilf!"

"You don't mean it!" Nat cried. "Sure, I'm from Kerry County, I'm proud to say! A darlin' place, a darlin' place!"

"Well, lads," the sergeant said to his squad, "tis plain this bhoy is no rebel up to divilmint. We'll be turnin' him loose, I'm thinkin'."

Nat grinned and started to put out his hand.

"One moment there, Sergeant," a cold nasal voice knifed from the darkness. "I'd like a look at your prisoner before you release him. There's something rings familiar about his voice."

A tall, dapper silhouette came from the night shadows, beckoning to a man behind him to bring up a bull's-eye lantern. All Nat could make out of the newcomer was that

he wore his right arm in a sling. But obviously he was a
Loyalist officer.

The lantern was brought up and the shutter was thrown
open to bathe Nat in a sickly orange light. He turned toward
the officer with his eyes narrowed against the glare.

"Ahh! You haven't caught an Irishman from Kerry
County, Sergeant. You've caught Nathaniel Towne, rebel
spy from Boston. The day of reckoning, eh, Towne?"
Lieutenant Ralston Morbes grinned at Nat like a cat grinning at a mouse hole.

13

MAYBE THE WORLD
IS A PRISON

From the barred window of his cell in Stone Jail, Nat could see the green-grown islets in the bay. They seemed so close, so vividly near, that he could almost reach between the bars and touch them.

He pulled back a step from the window and looked around at his sorry prison. The huge stone blocks were damp and lichenous, the flooring was foul with stale straw and rats' litter and the overspill of the slop bucket. He looked down at the shackles that held his ankles eighteen inches apart with their heavy link chain. And for a moment —because the islands were so rich with summer verdure, so clean and green and near—he thought he would start to yell. But he swallowed the impulse. He didn't want to become like Gibby Jones from the strain of prolonged imprisonment; not that Gibby yelled . . . no, it was something worse.

Two and a half weeks and I'm ready to start yelling, he thought apprehensively. *What will I be like after a year of this? Like Gibby.*

His cellmate was Gibson Jones, a merchantman skipper who had made the mistake of trying to run the port blockade on June 2, 1774, in his cargo brig *Alois*. Gibby had been paying for that mistake for twelve and one-half months, which was just about six months beyond the limit of his mental capability.

Sometime before Nat's arrival in Stone Jail, Gibby had cracked—as many men do from close confinement. He wasn't howling mad by any means, but he was definitely odd. Usually he would stay in his own dark corner and make little whisk brooms out of the old bits of rank straw. But sometimes he would get the chuckles. When this happened, he would giggle and chortle and hold his stomach and rock back and forth for an hour or more. And he would watch Nat with a sly, bright gleam in his eye, as though he were the possessor of a secret of which Nat knew nothing.

Nat hated these strange chuckly moods of Gibby's. They were downright creepy.

Nat shuffled across the straw-strewn floor and sat down heavily with his back to the wall that was always damp. Absently he watched Gibby at work on a new broom.

Two and a half weeks he had been rotting in Stone Jail, and not once had he been interrogated. No trial, no judgment or sentence, nothing. Ralston and his Tories had turned him over to the British, and he had been placed in this cell with Gibby and that was that.

Perhaps, he thought, *Ral knows he has no way of proving his accusation that I'm a spy. So maybe I'm just a prisoner of war—and will remain one until the war ends. If it ever does.*

He supposed he would have to create a hobby for himself to help the slow passage of time—like Gibby and his brooms. Maybe he could catch a couple of mice and teach them tricks. Or perhaps he should attempt the impossible task of deciphering the Abenaki message. The British had taken his brace of pistols, but no one had thought to search his person. He slipped the roll of birchbark from his shirt and looked at it wonderingly. It still remained a total blank to him. Or better yet (rather than teaching tricks to mice or studying Abenaki), perhaps he should direct his mental energies toward devising the means for escape. How was it that the young lover had escaped from his prison in *Manon Lescaut?* Something to do with a pistol as he recalled. And that possibility was out.

Suddenly his mind side-stepped back to the Loyalist girl he had met at the shack in the woods. He recalled her face, the way she had looked at him from her blond mist of hair. She had been pretty, quietly pretty . . . .

"I've got to get out of here," he said abruptly, unconsciously.

Gibby looked up from his manipulations with the wisps of straw.

"What say?"

"Gibby, in the year you've been here, haven't you figured out *any* method of escape?"

"Escape? Escape?" Gibby seemed to be tasting the word experimentally. "You mean outside? You want to get outside?"

"Of course. To get out of this stinking prison and rejoin the American army."

"American what? Whose army?"

Nat sighed. "Gibby, I've already explained to you what happened at Concord and Lexington. You haven't forgotten, have you? About how we have an army now, and how we've surrounded Boston?"

"Y-e-s . . . the army. You want to leave here and go fight with this army?"

"Certainly. Don't you?"

Gibby's eyes glowered down to two little pinpoints of light. Then he started to chuckle throatily.

"Gibby, for grab's sake, don't start *that* again!"

Gibby dropped his chuckle abruptly and popped his eyes wide open.

"Start what?"

"Oh, never mind," Nat replied wearily. *I've definitely got to get out of here . . . .*

He looked toward the window and saw that the glow had gone out of the grilled patch of sky. Another day gone, he thought. He rolled over and picked up his spoon and made a mark on the wall beside the seventeen marks that were already there. It was the fifteenth of June.

The clatter and iron-bound clang of doors opening in the corridor sounded, followed by the heavy-footed scrunch of boots. Time for the evening meal. The door to their cell swung open and a tallow candle chased the gathering shadows back into webby brown corners. Sergeant Hay, the Cockney sergeant of the guard, entered and beamed at Nat.

" 'Ere, is this any w'y to meet an hofficer? Oy've brung along a major to see you, oy 'ave!"

"A major?" Nat's interest perked up. "Who is he?"

A dapper line officer stepped around Sergeant Hay's elbow and into the light of the candle. He set his arms akimbo and grinned at Nat.

"Majaw William Dawes of the King's Own, Nat-o me lad!"

"Billy!" Nat got up and tried to run to his friend and nearly took a header because of the blame leg irons.

"What's this? Irons on my friend? I'm afraid I'll have to take you to task, Sergeant Hay," Billy admonished the beaming sergeant.

"Oy've the remedy for that, sir," Hay announced, and he took a key from his pocket and hunkered down to release Nat's fetter-sore legs. Nat was still staring at Billy with open-mouthed amazement.

"Where did you get the uniform?"

"From your old pal Benny Frazer. It's a stage costume. Don't look at it too hard or it falls apart. Also have a boat cloak and an officer's hat for you. Friend Benny was more than eager to supply my needs—after I'd mentioned to him the possibility of having his theater visited by a Boston mob if he didn't."

Sergeant Hay reached inside his tunic and produced two familiar looking pistols. "Oy believe these belong to you, laddy buck."

Nat took Major Pitcairn's weapons and looked at them for a moment speculatively. Funny the way these pistols seemed to cling to him—almost as if for an inexorable purpose.

"What about 'im?" Hay wagged his key toward Gibby, who was crouching back in the shadows and watching the group by the door with nervously fluttering eyes.

"He goes too," Nat said, turning back into the cell. "C'mon, Gibby. We're getting out of here."

"Out?" Gibby whispered. "Outside?" He drew further back along the wall. "Go out there? Oh—no—no. Not outside. Outside is a prison. Everyone who is outside is a prisoner. And—and I—I'm their jailor!" Then he started to giggle and chuckle.

Sergeant Hay tapped his temple with the key. "Bats in the belfry."

"I don't know," Billy said with his usual grin. "Maybe he's got something there."

Maybe he does, Nat thought soberly. *Maybe the world is a prison. And maybe that's why we're here—to force open the gates and knock down the walls.* "So long, Gibby," he said quietly.

Gibby chuckled throatily and pulled farther into the shadows, like a soulless animal that understands suffering but has no knowledge of man's hope for an eternal destiny.

Sergeant Hay, it would seem, was an ambitious man. For some time he had been selling information to the Committee of Safety, and he had agreed to help Billy spring Nat from Stone Jail with the understanding that Billy and Nat would take him with them to the American headquarters, introduce him to Ward and Warren, present to them his military qualifications, and enable him to secure an officer's commission in the army.

"Oy'm about to become an American, Oy am," he confided in Nat, as the three of them hurried across the darkened courtyard. "No fat old king is going to shove *me* around the rest of moy bally life!"

"Well, if we don't get to General Ward in a hurry—Gage will be shoving all of us around," Billy muttered, herding his two companions through an open gate and into an ill-lit street.

"Why? What's up?" Nat wanted to know.

"Hay here got the word from higher up that Burgoyne has talked old stick-in-the-mud Gage into making a decisive move. Gage has passed orders to seize and fortify Dorchester Heights and the Charlestown peninsula. The operation is supposed to commence on the eighteenth."

"Then it looks like I got out of quod just in time," Nat said.

Billy laughed. "Yeah—to get yourself shot full of holes."

Gluing themselves to the shadows, the three fugitives made their way down to the shore of the Charles River, and Billy led the way to a small boat hidden in the tall weed.

"We'll pull over to Lechmere's Point," Billy whispered, "and——"

"Not yet, we won't," Hay hissed with a sudden urgency. "Down! Get down! There's a giddy patrol boat."

The three men crouched in suspense around the boat as, over the top of the weed, Nat saw a patrol barge rowing

slowly by in the starlight. There were six men at the oars, a sergeant on the lookout in the bow and an ensign muffled in his boat cloak in the stern.

Quite distinctly the three fugitives heard the sergeant call: "Sir! I saw a movement in the tules there."

"Where away?"

"Right there where the weed humps the highest, sir."

"Well, give them a hail. Starboard—backwater!"

"Hoy! Who's there! You in the weeds! Stand and name yourself!"

Nat took in his breath, looking across the gunwale at Billy's star-bright eyes. Billy's teeth flashed at him in the dark.

"Playing possum with us, sir. Shall I order a volley?"

Sergeant Hay gasped and started to turn away from the boat in a crouch. Nat caught him by the arm and held him. Then he tipped up his head and gave a mournful whistle, imitating to a T the cry of a killdeer. He caught handfuls of weeds and shook them to and fro, and whistled again. They clearly heard the ensign's scornful laugh.

"There's your rebels, Sergeant. A confounded plover in the weeds! Carry on, for gad's sake."

Nat and his two friends watched the barge pull slowly away, growing smaller and more buglike as it crawled across the star-shot surface of the river shallows. Sergeant Hay let out his breath.

"C'mon, chums. This ar'n't such a healthy plyce to be. Let's get over to the other side where us Americans belong!"

14

ARE THEY FIGHTIN' THIS BATTLE, OR ARE WE?

Nat tried three times that morning to gain an audience with General Ward at Command Headquarters; but the multitude of harassed aide-de-camps, clerks, couriers, and staff officers—all as busy as bees in a kicked-over-hive—were too much for him to cope with. He'd lost track of Billy at Cambridge, and Sergeant Hay had gone off to a tavern with the ambiguous promise from some red-sashed colonel that they would see what they could do about getting him the command of a company, later on.

He couldn't reach Ward, couldn't find Warren, and had no idea where Old Put was. And no one else seemed at all interested in the roll of birchbark he was still carrying. No one had time to worry about Indians; much bigger things were afoot—though exactly *what*, no one was quite sure. Nat gave up and returned to Hollis Hall to find Shad.

"Shucks, Natty," Shad said, "you wouldn't get anywhere with Ward, even if you was to reach him. He don't know beans about Injuns, and what's more he don't care to know.

169

He's runnin' hisself in circles with the redcoats he's got on his hands right here. Old Put is who you should see about Injuns."

"But I can't find him. By draggit, Shad, this Abenaki message has to have *some* importance to it; look at all the trouble Jessie went to to get possession of it."

"Sure it's got importance. But right now the most important thing to this army is the news Billy brought about Gage wanting to take Dorchester and Charlestown. I don't know what old Artemas Ward is planning to do about it, but look around you—he's sure plannin' to do something!"

Shad had his recruits grouped around a table and was teaching them how to roll cartridges with coarse black gunpowder and the pages of a book he had "picked up" somewhere. Nat looked at the powder the recruits had been issued. As far as he could see no man had more than a gill to make cartridges with.

"Where's the rest of your powder? You couldn't lick rabbits with only a quarter of a pint per man."

"Don't I know it?" Shad said angrily. "But this was all they'd give us. Said it was all they had. Cat's backside! The Delawares take more'n this with 'em when they leave the tepee to go down to the crick for a drink a water!"

"You think we're really going to fight then, Sergeant?" a youth asked.

"Fight? You bet your left boot we're gonna fight! I don't know what or where, but I've heard that whatever it is, old Artemas has put Prescott and Put in charge of it. And there's two fellas you can always count on for *one* thing: both of 'em are always spoilin' for a scrap!"

Nat happened to glance at a page Shad had just torn from his book, and his eye was caught by a line from Edmund Burke:

. . . new men will come in, and not improbably with new ideas; at this very instant the causes productive of such a change are strongly at work.

At this very instant . . . it gave him a funny feeling, that. Symbolic.

At sunset the drums began a sharp *rat-ta-tat*, and Nat and Shad fell out with Knowton's company and fell in on the parade ground. Everywhere you could hear voices asking the same question: *What's up? Where we going?* But no one seemed to know—at least not for sure. You heard all sorts of answers working through the ranks: Dorchester—Charlestown—Chelsea—Roxbury—Jamaica Plain—Bunker's Hill . . . .

As far as Nat could see, the uniform of the army hadn't changed a mite since the day two months ago when the minutemen had faced the British at Lexington. Ragged homespun was still the order of the day. Even Massachusetts' prize colonel, William Prescott, was dressed like a simple farmer. The only symbol of authority he wore was a pencil-thin rapier stuck in his belt. Personally Nat would hate to ward off a British bayonet thrust with a brittle weapon like that!

Not that the granddaddy musket *he* had been issued was anything to crow over. His secret conviction was that the ancient wheellock had been along on Frontenac's expedition against the Iroquois in 1696. It would probably blow off both his hands at the first shot—if it would blow at all.

General Ward, looking sick and melancholy, was talking to a group of officers some distance away. Nat recognized Generals Putnam and Frye, and Colonels Bridge, Gerrish, Gridley, and Prescott. All at once Old Put broke out of the group with a rosy beam on his pumpkin face, and walked away rubbing his hands together energetically.

"All right, boys! Let's move 'em out. We got work to do tonight!"

In the gathering dusk the Yankees trooped by the wide, boulder-pegged fields with their bordering hedgerows, passing shabby little farms that sat in an orbit of hens and shoats and ducks, children too; all crowding up to the edge of the road to watch the soldiers march.

Some companies, Nat noticed, looked as though they were starting on an expedition: marching with blanket rolls and haversacks, with cooking kettles knocking on their hips. Others carried picks and spades.

"Looks like we're gonna fortify something," was Shad's observation.

And the farther they went along the road the more it looked as though Charlestown peninsula was meant to be the destination. And more and more now the words "Bunker Hill" kept being passed back through the ranks.

Night came upon the march, and the thousand or so men straggled along the road in a careless route-step, taking frequent breaks whenever they felt like it, smoking their pipes and swapping chaws of tobacco and passing water bottles around. No one seemed to be in much of a hurry.

At Charlestown Neck the army met Putnam again. He was waiting with some wagons nearly spilling over with fascines, gabions, empty barrels, and entrenching tools. Another break was ordered while the officers went into a huddle with Old Put. NCO's moved through the shuffling men, admonishing them to keep their fat mouths shut, to hold down the noise.

On a stubby knoll Nat found two men in a quiet argument.

"I still say yer a fool to go into this business when yer a married man! What of yer widder and chilren if you get kilt?"

"Listen!" the married man said vehemently. "*You're* the fool! Any soldier that risks his life without ever having been married or had children don't *know* about life! Because you can't know life till you know *love*. Tis the secret of life. And I'll leave it to this fella here," turning to Nat in the dark. "What about it, brother?"

"Love?" Nat said emptily, and again his mind side-slipped to the activated imagery of the Loyalist girl standing on the porch of the shanty in the far-away woods. "Love?" he said softly. "I—I'm afraid I know nothing about love. I never had time to get around to it."

"You didn't, huh?" the married man said with sudden quiet compassion. "Well, son, let's hope the redcoats let you live long enough to find the time."

Nat, saying nothing more, shouldered his heavy musket and went down into the road again.

Love . . . he wondered. Then he raised his head. Far off across the Charlestown Neck the black and bald hulks of Bunker and Breed's hills showed against the navy-blue sky. Waiting.

The passage across the Neck was slow, delayed by numerous jam-ups. The Neck was only forty feet wide with clots of seaweed and bumps of black rock on either beach, and one of Gridley's cannons had gotten into trouble. Nat could hear the artillerymen swearing blue murder as he edged by a fascine-loaded wagon and onto the peninsula proper.

Knowlton was reorganizing his company at the foot of Bunker Hill. Not far off Old Put was in an argument with

Prescott, Gridley, Frye, and two Massachusetts colonels, Bridge and Brickett. They were standing in a field by the cart road that ran between the two treeless hills.

"Bunker Hill stinks!" Old Put was raging. "From Breed's Hill we can command Boston city itself! But all we can command from Bunker is a bunch of milk cows!"

"But Breed's Hill can be flanked, you old fool!" Frye cried.

"*Flanked?* You talk about flankin'—what do you think will happen to Bunker if Gage decides to land troops on the Neck behind us? By draggit, they can *both* be flanked, if it comes to that. What do you say, Will?"

Prescott didn't know what to say. "All I can say is I'm in favor of holding the position that will be the most advantageous to us."

"And that's *Breed's!*"

"Now hold on, Put," Gridley came in. "I'll admit that Breed's is better situated for artillery, but how are you going to get around the Committee of Safety's orders? Those orders are explicit: to raise a strong redoubt on Bunker Hill, and to———"

"And to hogwash!" Old Put raged. "I don't give a dead frog for the Committee's orders! Are *they* here? Are they fightin' this battle, or are we?"

"Nevertheless, an order is an order and———"

"All right! All right! You want to fortify Bunker Hill? Fine! *I'll* fortify it. And Prescott will fortify Breed's. But by grab, we're gonna fortify Breed's *first!*"

Knowlton was moving through the dark shapes of his men, calling, "Towne. Where's Towne?" Nat stepped forward with a salute.

"Take ten men, Towne, and fall in with Captain Nut-

ting's Massachusetts company. You're going into Charlestown to watch the enemy's movements."

Nat selected his men and reported to Captain Nutting.
The Connecticutters fell in with the Massachusetts company, and they cut obliquely across the damp field where the
officers were now breaking up their discussion, and headed
toward the Charles shore.

Nat could see the mill pond off on his right glimmering
like a giant's mirror, and, beyond the causeway, the two
black shapes of the British floating batteries. He couldn't
see any men-of-war as yet.

As quietly as possible the Yankees infiltrated the nearly
deserted village. Nutting sent one detachment to the right,
to a small copse of wood that sheltered the school, sent
another detachment straight through the town to the docks,
and ordered Nat to take his men to a pear orchard just
beyond the town.

Stumbling, lurching across the rutty earth, the squad entered the orchard and started flickering through the crazy-
quilt pattern thrown by the tree shadows. Approaching the
shore, they hunkered down in a loose line and stared across
the water at Boston in its sleeping serenity.

"Corporal! I can make out the men-o'-war. Over to your
left."

Nat went forward in a crouch and hunkered down again.
A cold tingling tiptoed up his spine when he looked at the
tall black shapes of the King's ships, seemingly so close he
could pelt them with rocks.

"Know 'em?" the boy on his right asked.

"Yeah," Nat whispered, and started pointing. "Sloop
Lively, twenty guns; sloop *Falcon*, sixteen; armed transport
Symmetry, eighteen; frigate *Glasgow*, twenty-four; and that

monster out there's the *Somerset*, ship of the line, sixty-eight guns."

The boy let out his breath raspingly. "Say—that's a gol-dummed lot a cannons against what *we* got; when you throw in them two floating batteries of theirs as well."

Nat grinned. "Don't forget to throw in the guns on Copp's Hill over in Boston too."

There was nothing much to do except wait. A couple of the men curled up for a doze. Someone was passing a water bottle around. Nat propped himself against an old log and watched the shifting water and the men-of-war. Now and then he heard a distant *dok* as a pick struck a rock, and sometimes the scroop of a shovel biting in. Once he heard the *Lively's* watch call the half-hour All's well; and the boy beside him chuckled. "That's what you think, brother."

It was the hour before dawn when a runner came slipping through the interlaced shadows of the grove, calling: "Towne. Cap'n says if you've anything to report, to take it up to Prescott on the hill."

Nat didn't have much—except the names and armament of the men-of-war facing the redoubt on Breed's Hill—but he was looking for an excuse for activity, so he decided to take what he had up the hill.

Colonel Gridley the engineer (not Major Gridley the artillery commander) had laid out the ground plan for the redoubt. It was a very simple affair, really: three-sided, each earth wall about 150 feet long, with the open end facing Bunker Hill. A small triangular redan had been set in the frontal wall, and two gun platforms were being constructed for this same wall.

The Connecticut and Massachusetts farmer-militia were not, perhaps, the best soldiers in the world, but one thing they were the best at was digging. They felt right at home with picks and shovels in their work-grained hands, and within a matter of four hours they had raised the walls of the redoubt to six feet; this included an inner fire-step, plus an outer ditch, or small dry moat.

The night was hot, and many of the men toiled naked to the waist in the fading, star-dusty light. Even Prescott had shed his coat and wig, and you could see his bald head moving energetically along the walls. Everyone was calling for water, and they were beginning to wonder where in blue Hades was their relief, not to mention reinforcements. As Nat approached the Massachusetts colonel, he heard Gridley say:

"You've been sold out, Will. Ward isn't about to send reinforcements. He's too blame scared that Gage will take this opportunity to make a sortie against Cambridge. And you were a saphead to have let Old Put talk you into fortifying this hill. You can't possibly hold it. One British charge and you're through!"

"Colonel," Prescott said coolly, "you can rant and rave all you wish, but Putnam ordered me to hold this hill, and by heaven I will! To the last man, if it comes to that."

"Well at least send back these men and have Put send up your relief. These farmers are beat out from digging all night."

But Prescott shook his head, turning away. "No. The men who have raised this redoubt are the best able to defend it. They have the merit of the labor, and now they'll have the honor of the victory. Colonel Bridge! Look here a moment!"

The colonel had enough on his mind without Nat bothering him about ships. He moved along the dark, sweating shapes of the Connecticut men working on the east wall until he found Shad.

"Natty! You been keepin' out a trouble for a change?" Shad demanded. "By grab, boy, I've near worked my mitts off tonight! You know what? These farmboys don't know barrel from butt on a muskit; but you just hand 'em a shovel and can they sling the dirt around!"

Captain Knowlton strolled by with a tight smile. "Better hold on to your hats, boys," he said, and he nodded toward the east, where the sun was commencing to jack up the lid of the horizon.

Dawn was established. The green-garbed western land took on depth and dimension, humping into mounds and eroded systems of fat little hills cut separate by white scars of sand, where the spring water had flowed. Then the true hills began. They rolled away in the diurnal light and became lost in the retreating darkness.

Almost on the heels of the first milky glint of dawn the bosun pipes aboard the *Lively* began to shrill frantically.

Weeeeee-weep! Weeeeee-weep!

"Now we'll catch the old nick," Shad growled.

Antlike, from the vantage point of the Yankees on the hill, the seamen aboard the *Lively* ran out a long gun and let the Charlestown peninsula have a ball. *Pa-lowm!* The heavy blam of the retort shivered and resounded in the misty air of the warm June morning. The *Lively*, businesslike, swung on her sheet cable and, as her starboard came to bear, she erupted a blinding broadside on Breed's Hill.

The thick, vibrant sound of the guns hurried across the Charles, up the steps of the wharves and down through the sullen shadows of the sleeping city. The citizens, loyal and nonloyal, and the men of the British army sat up in their beds and cots with a start and every face wore the same question. *What? For gad's sake, what?*

But the men on Breed's Hill knew very well what was up—their number. The cannonballs came slamming, thudding into the side of the hill, and some of them bounced upward, spinning smoke, and took off again.

Nat hit the dirt with the rest of the rebels, and many looked as though they would just as soon maintain that position for the remainder of the day, while a few panicked and sprang up and started to run down the back of the hill.

Nat raised his head and looked around. He couldn't believe what he saw. Instead of berating his men for cowards, or beseeching them not to pay any mind to the cannonballs —Colonel Prescott had elected to give them a silent sight lesson. He was casually strolling along the top of the earth parapet, in full view of the enemy ships!

Shad springing up from the ground, yelled, "If Willy Prescott can stand up there like a bull's-eye painted on a barn door, *we* can at least work behint this fat old fort of ours!"

The Yankees began picking up their shovels and picks and themselves. Two aides (looking rather white around the gills) joined Prescott in his stroll along the top of the parapet. Work was resumed.

Meanwhile Admiral Graves (presumably tearing his wig to shreds because he didn't know what all the hubbub was about) signaled the *Lively* to shut her fat-cannon mouth, so that he could get a full grasp on the situation. A great deal of time was wasted—valuable time for the Americans, who were busy strengthening their redoubt—as longboats were pulled from ship to ship and flag signals run up and down the halyards with no end of announcements.

Finally—after it had been carefully pointed out to the admiral that the pesky rabble had fortified Breed's Hill with a sturdy redoubt and were raising gun platforms—Graves ordered the *Lively, Falcon,* and *Somerset* to commence firing.

Broadside after broadside slammed home, cannonballs going *wwwwhosh* overhead, as niners, twelvers, twenty-four pounders came screaming across the water, whacked into the weedy slope of Breed's face, and went off on gaudy ricochets.

A Captain Bancroft felt one whizz so close over his left shoulder that he thought his left eye had gone along with it. He hobbled around in a painful circle clutching his eye, muttering: "Gol dummit! That'll cost 'em! I'll make 'em pay for that eye!" And another ball abruptly sheared off the head of one of Prescott's aides. The decapitated officer went down in a crumple, spattering Prescott with his gore.

Some of the Yankees started to panic when they saw what had happened to the aide. "What'll we do? What'll we do?" they wailed.

Prescott, calmly cleaning his scarlet hands with fresh dirt, glanced at them. "Do? Why, bury him, of course. What else?"

Nat was pleased to see Dr. Warren coming up the back of the hill, smartly dressed in a fine silk-fringed waistcoat. Because the doctor was now a major general, Prescott offered him command of the hill.

"Wouldn't think of it, Colonel. I'm only here as a volunteer."

Colonel Gridley came over to shake Warren's hand, and to ask, "What do you think of our position here, General?"

Warren and the two colonels looked around them in the light of day and what they saw was not the most promising sight in the world. A small earth redoubt perched all by itself on a bald hilltop. No outworks or support for the flanks. Perhaps 1,200 untrained, undisciplined troops milling around the hill.

"We-ll," Warren said musingly, "for one thing, it looks as though a British landing party could flank you without much difficulty. It might be advisable to construct a breastwork along your left here to protect that side of your redoubt."

"That's good," Prescott agreed instantly. "I don't have too much fear for my right flank. I've got Little's regiment and Nutting's company holding Charlestown. Now about this left flank . . . "

They weren't the only officers with problems. . . .

In one of the upstairs rooms of the Province House over in Boston, Gage was holding a council of war. Principal in this group were Generals Howe, Clinton, and Burgoyne.

Clinton said: "An immediate landing with five hundred troops, directly on the Charlestown Neck. We will have the rabble on Breed's Hill cut off entirely. At the same time we will make a frontal landing on the hill. Gentlemen, we will have them in a perfect box!"

Gage said: "I disagree, General. It is not a sound military practice to interpose a force between two bodies of the enemy; in this case, I refer to the rabble on the hill and the remainder of the rebel army on the mainland. I am in favor of a landing on Morton's Point. We will march our troops up the east side along the Mystic, flank the redoubt, and strike it from the rear."

Clinton said (nearly cried): "But, General, the Neck is so simple!"

Howe said: "Gentlemen, please! We are wasting time. General Gage is quite correct in his approach to the problem. This is not a battle. We are not on the fields of Europe now. We are simply confronted with a foolish rabble who have armed themselves with broomsticks and pruning knives. All we need to disperse them is a troop movement and a show of arms."

Burgoyne said: "But we could capture them lock, stock, and barrel if you two gentlemen would only listen to reason! They have marched into a trap. If we hurry to the Neck there is no possible way for them to escape from the peninsula. We'll break the back of this confounded rebellion today!"

Gage said: "General, as I've already pointed out, your way might possibly mean that our troops would find themselves hampered by a crossfire. Whereas if we do it *my* way, we will simply march around the hill from Morton's Point and either chase them all away or take them prisoner. One way or another is beside the point. The object is to show this rabble once and for all that they are foolhardy to think of standing up to British regulars. Why, it is beyond comprehension that any force in the world could make a stand against the Royal Army! And the idea of these clodhoppers on the hill attempting such folly reminds me of a bayonet trying to fight a cannon!"

Howe said: "Believe me, General, the only casualties that will be realized from this day's trivial work will be on the rebels' score—as they run all over each other trying to escape!"

Gage asked: "You don't think, General, that they will actually attempt to stand up to British regulars?"

And Burgoyne replied, thoughtfully: "No, sir, I don't think they will. Still—they're strange people, these Americans, with unusual leaders. Very unusual."

But General Gage had his way. And General Howe drew the short straw. He was to lead the landing on Morton's Point.

The long morning dragged on, and still the rabble on the hill toiled at their fortification under the sullen bombardment of the men-of-war and the Copp's Hill Battery—a bombardment that could be heard as far away as Braintree Village, where an Abigail Adams held the hand of an eight-year-old boy who would one day become the sixth President of the United States.

Abigail and her son listened to the distant iron-bound thunder, and the mother wondered if the day—perhaps the decisive day—had come, on which the fate of America depended.

15

WAR WASN'T A TIDY OFFICER
DYING SERENELY...

On Boston Common the reg-
ulars were being fed, inspected, and berated as usual and in
general. To Major Pitcairn, passing by with his orders, it
must have seemed like any other army day. His favorite
sergeant, Pat Mahoney, had his marines lined in the boiling
heat of the green. The marines, under the weight of their
uniforms, eighty-pound field packs, twelve-pound Tower
muskets, looked wan and miserable. Their bright scarlet
coats were dark with deep sweat stains.

Mahoney stood before them, his square fists resting on
his thick hips, his beefy face red and pouty, his voice harsh
as the bite of a cat-o'-nine tails. Major Pitcairn paused in
the shade to watch.

"Nah then, me buckos," Mahoney rasped at his patient
charges. " 'Tis not a demn I give about what ye've heard
today, 'cause *none* of it tis true! The truth is that General
Gage has planned a bit of an outing for yez over in the
Charlestown meadows. In a moment tis down to the harbor
we'll go. There the General has some boats awaitin' yez;

and we'll be after taking a bit of a pleasure cruise across the Charles, so we will! Ye'll mind that ye're British regulars; yez won't open yer big Irish yaps and shout at the lassies. 'Tis gintlemen ye'll be! Do ye catch me, O'Hara?"

"Yis, Sergeant."

"Once on the other side the General will be after givin' uz a picnic. Ye'll mind yer manners, the lot of yez! And not make any mess. Are ye still with me, O'Hara?"

"Yis, Sergeant."

"After our snack we'll all take uz a little stroll up to the top of yon hill called Breed's—saints persarve uz, what a name! And we'll see what thim farmer lads have been about."

"Will we be after fightin' thim farmer lads now, Sergeant?"

Mahoney rubbed at his moist face with a pudgy hand and turned to Pitcairn with a look of patient sorrow. The major swallowed a smile.

"O'Hara!" Mahoney cried in a voice that trembled on violence. "How, man, can yez be standin' there askin' me that? When we reach the top of the hill, where will the farmer lads be, I'm askin' yez? Running home to their mithers, that's where! Do ye think now they'll be standin' up to British regulars?"

"No, Sergeant," replied the sheepish O'Hara.

Major Pitcairn grinned openly and turned away. Mahoney, of course, was right; there wasn't an army in Europe that could stand up against British regulars. Why, everyone knew that the moment the famous redcoats marched upon the field the enemy—no matter who—was fifty per cent licked, morally speaking. Still—the major remembered the long bloody retreat along the Lexington-Concord road.

That was one day on which the "farmer lads" had not run home to their mothers. He had lost a fine pair of pistols that day too. Probably in the hands of some clod-footed farmboy right now . . .

In the heavy heat of noon the regulars filed down the wharves and into the barges. The sun was a whorling glassy ball of lemon fire, and the thick air quivered and moaned under the continuous strain of the guns.

A small caliber shell whanged out of the redoubt on Breed's Hill and fell short in the torpid water, spitting up a flash of white two hundred yards before the foremost barge.

Corporal Nason said: "Hi! They've a bit of cannon up there."

Major Pitcairn watched the flung spray fall back onto the glassy surface of the river, and he smiled. Did the rebels think to scare them off with that? His eyes followed the gradual sweep of Breed's Hill as it rose before them. Still and all—it would be a warm march with full packs.

O'Hara's voice floated back from the bow.

"I tell yez I know thim farmer lads. 'Tis rum they fight on, if fight at all. Nah, whin we gain the top of yon hill, scatter out, I say, and see how many of thim rum barrels can we——"

"O'Hara!" Mahoney rasped. "Is it yer mouth I hear?"

But Major Pitcairn, sitting relaxed in the stern, smiled lazily, his eyes glittering with water reflection, and said: "Don't be too hard on them, Sergeant. They will taste glory today."

General Howe mothered his 28 barges ashore and landed nearly 1,550 infantry, grenadiers, artillerymen, plus twelve pieces of field cannon in the first two waves. The regulars were lined along the beach of Morton's Point and in the meadows fronting Breed's Hill, and in the blaze of early afternoon they sweltered and waited while Howe reconnoitered the American position.

The physical aspect of the rebel defense was suddenly viewed in a new light. Howe gathered his staff in a group, and for the first time there could be detected a subtle hesitation in his manner.

"Feed the troops," he ordered. "We'll wait for reinforcements."

From the redoubt and the hastily constructed breastwork on Breed's Hill the bushed, dirty, shirtsleeved Americans watched the gaudy spectacle of the British embarkation, and it was a sight so vividly magnificent that no one in America had ever seen its equal. The flower of the King's army was coming in two parallel lines of single file across the Charles River. With their scarlet coats and steel bayonets and brass fieldpieces the armada of 28 barges glittered and sparked like the jewel box of a queen.

As the barges pulled into Mortons Point, Shad let out his breath.

"*Wheew!* I wouldn't believe it if I warn't seein' it with my own eyes! Gage had us in a box but he's left the lid open. I tell you, Natty, if Washington had been leadin' those redcoats they'd a gone smack to the Neck and cut us off cold! Why even a French ensign or a Mingo sachem would've done the same. You can travel far and wide, but you ain't *never* gonna find peawits like you'll find right here at home in the regular army! No sir! British officer peawits is the *best* peawits of all. I've always said so and I'll go on sayin' it!"

Captain Knowlton was shouting for his company to fall in.

"Knowlton's company! Shake a leg! We're pulling out."

Hastily the two hundred men fell into disorganized ranks, as Knowlton came tramping along their front.

"Towne! Where's that actor?"

"Right here, sir." Nat held up his hand.

"Towne, we're going down to that rail fence in the marsh. Prescott wants us to fortify his left flank. But I want you to continue acting as my runner. You'll keep communications open between the fence and the redoubt. Got that?" He didn't wait for Nat's answer but swung away to shout at Prescott.

"Colonel! Gridley's cannons aren't going to do a thing against an uphill infantry attack. Will you let me have them down at the fence?"

Prescott waved his hand and turned to Gridley the artillery commander (not Gridley the engineer) who had fetched up four six-pounders by oxen and horses. Gridley and a Captain Callender ordered their men to grab the dragropes, and the fieldpieces were yanked out of the redoubt in a fervor akin to panic. That was the last the Connecticutters saw of Gridley the artilleryman.

Nat and Shad tramped down the back of Breed's Hill with Knowlton's company and formed in a marshy meadow near the foot of Bunker Hill. A stone and rail fence, not more than waist-high, stretched from Breed's Hill to the bank of the Mystic River. It was about two hundred yards long, and how Knowlton could hope to hold it with only two hundred men was beyond everyone's imagination.

"All right, boys," Knowlton said. "We don't have much to work with here, but if we pull down the rails from that fence adjacent to us and reset it about ten feet in front of our stone wall, and plug the space in between the two with hay and new-cut grass, we might make it *look* like quite a formidable breastwork."

So they did it, working feverishly to gather the newly cut grass laying everywhere underfoot, which disturbed the browsing cows even more than the clang-banging shells.

"*Coo!* Boss, *coo!*" Shad shouted at the heifers. "Git out a here afore you get yourselves hurt. This ain't no place for man nor beast!"

"Sergeant Holly!" Knowlton yelled. "Will you kindly leave those milkers alone and pay attention to business? I want you to take a squad of men midway between this fence and the breastwork and dig three flèches—that is to say three V-shaped trenches!"

"Cap," Shad shouted back, "I was diggin' flèches at the Forks a the Ohio to fight off Mingos with when you was still sayin' *Goo-goo* at your ma! I know what to do."

As Shad took off up the slope of Breed's Hill, an enthusiastic shout went up from the Connecticut troops behind the rail fence.

"Hi, boys! Here comes old Seth!"

Nat looked around and saw a granddaddy so old and skinny and crabbed he must have been seventy if he was a day. It was old General Seth Pomeroy crippling across the field for all he was worth, toting over his scrawny shoulder a musket he had made himself and used in 1745 at the siege of Louisburg.

"Hi, Cap'n!" old Seth yelled at Knowlton. "You got room for one more along this fence a yorn? I rid me a borried horse up to the Neck, but the fire from them floatin' batteries there is so heavy I didn't have the heart to submit him to it. So I been on foot ever since! I already been all the way up Bunker Hill, but them cowards there ain't fixin' to see them no fightin'; so now I've come along to you! Don't reckon I can go much further. I'm some winded, I am!"

"General," Knowlton said with a broad grin, "we welcome you with open arms! What's the situation at the Neck? Any reinforcements yet?"

"Reinforcements!" cried the granddaddy of generals. "Those scurvy cowards back at the Neck is so a-scairt of the battery fire they wouldn't cross over was the British to be firin' gold pieces a eight at 'em! *No* you ain't gittin' no reinforcements—'ceptin' John Stark's New Hampshire regiment. Now there you got some American fightin' men! When they heard they was going to march, they cut the lead for their bullets right out of the organ pipes of a Cambridge church!"

"But how *many* men is he bringing, General?" Knowlton implored the old fellow.

"How do I know? A regiment—whatever that means in this gol-dummit army. But I'll say this for Stark: he didn't let that raking fire at the Neck hold him back no more'n it did me! He marched his men across just as if the floatin' batteries was firin' powder puffs at him instead a cannonballs!"

About that time Captain Callender jockeyed his two six-pounders up to the fence. Anyone could tell at a glance that something was bugging Callender. For one thing Gridley had ran out on him. For another Old Put had caught Callender trying to haul his cannons up Bunker Hill and had ordered him on threat of court martial to take his artillery to the rail fence, where Prescott had told him to go earlier.

"Here they are, Knowlton," Callender said, not meeting

the captain's eyes. "But we ain't got no ammo for 'em. It's all back on Bunker Hill. I'll get it up here right quick."

Knowlton said nothing as Callender pulled back in a greater panic than ever and disappeared. Knowlton, as well as his men, had an idea that if the British were to be stopped at the rail fence, it wouldn't be cannons that stopped them.

But the Connecticut company was cheered by the sight of Colonel Stark's New Hampshire men bearing down on them. Stark himself, tall and angular and as tough as a horseshoe with the nails rusty and bent over, led them by the rail fence, shouting:

"I already been on Bunker Hill and told that fat old Putnam I ain't about to take orders from no Connecticutter. And if I ain't takin' 'em from a general, I sure gawd ain't gonna take 'em from no captain! I know what's got to be done and I aim to do her!"

Knowlton smiled mildly, saying: "We're glad to see you, Stark. Even if you are a bit late."

Which nearly blew Stark sky-high. "You can go leap at the moon, Knowlton. Maybe we are late—but one *fresh* man is worth ten worn-out ones!" He pointed to where the rail fence ended at the river bank.

"And in case you Connecticut henheads ain't noticed, there's a strip of beach below you there that them redcoats can use to flank you. All right, boys, start gathering up rocks. We'll build our own wall!"

Nat was sent up the hill to report to Prescott. He saw that Shad's three small flèches were V-shaped, each one behind and slightly above the other. Shad waved his cocked hat at him excitedly.

"Hi, Natty! Who's that big man I see down there with Stark's men?"

"Major Andrew McClary. He led the raid at Portsmouth Castle in December to seize the King's powder and arms."

"Well, but just *how* big is he? He looks like seven feet from here."

"A couple of inches taller'n you, Shad. Fellas say he's the biggest man in the provincial army."

Shad wiped at his pursed lips and rammed his hat back on his head and reached for a pick. He didn't look one bit happy. It was a matter of pride with Shad that *he* should be the biggest man in the army.

Nat came across a portly, middle-aged gentleman who was dressed to the nines like a London fashion plate. He was a well-to-do Pennsylvania Dutchman, and he was toiling his weight up the hill with an expensive fowling piece over his shoulder.

"You, poy! Vere ist der fidting der most?" he called breathlessly.

Nat pointed. "I guess it'll be up at the redoubt, sir."

The Dutchman nodded his steaming red face. "Den dot's vhere ve go."

Prescott merely shrugged when Nat reported that Knowlton and Stark didn't have any cannons to help hold the fence. His big problems right now were men and powder; he simply didn't have enough of either. He couldn't be bothered about cannons.

"Tell Knowlton he'll have to do the best he can with what he's got. I'm just barely holding on to what men I have here by my eyeteeth. Even Bridge and Brickett, two of my *own* colonels, took one look at the British and claimed they had stomach cramps and ran off."

Later Nat was to hear that if it hadn't been for Prescott there would have been no redoubt, no defense, no fight on

Breed's Hill. It was through Prescott's energy, endurance, resolution, conviction, and courage that Americans owed their heritage for that decisive day.

From the hill Nat commanded a full view of the American defenses. The right wing was held by Little and Nutting's snipers in and around Charlestown; the center was the redoubt and breastwork held by Prescott; then Shad's three flèches, Knowlton's rail fence, and Stark's stone wall on the beach constituted the left wing.

Down on Morton's Point he could see Howe's regiments lining up: the Grenadiers, the Light Infantry, the Fifth, Thirty-eighth, Forty-third, and Fifty-second. Howe's reinforcements, the First Marines and the Forty-seventh, had landed near the pear orchard. It was nearly three in the afternoon when Nat started down the hill again.

General Pigot was Howe's second in command, and he was in charge of the British left wing—which meant that the snipers in Charlestown were giving him nothing but grief. Finally, in blind anger, he sent a request to Admiral Graves to do something about the rabble in the town. Graves responded instantly and eagerly by ordering his ships to bombard the town with hot shot and carcasses —hollow iron balls pierced with holes and containing combustibles.

This gave Little and Nutting's snipers a warm moment, but, as Charlestown caught on fire and began to cloud the sky with thick black pillars of smoke, it didn't drive them away. They simply abandoned the town and took up new positions in the orchard.

Howe wasn't a complete simpleton. He still thought his plan to flank the American left wing was feasible. He ordered Pigot to make a feint at Breed's Hill with the marines, the Thirty-eighth, Forty-third, and Forty-seventh; while he would march the Fifth and Fifty-second across the marsh to strike the rail fence, and the Grenadiers and Light Infantry would hit the stone wall on the beach. It was a cinch.

Nat paused on the hillside between the end of the breast-work and Shad's flèches as the sudden drum-roll rattled through the slam of the guns. He felt his heartbeat quicken, and he sank to his knees in the weeds, watching.

The officers wheeled the regulars into a long battle line of two ranks, and the advance was ordered. You could hear the omnipresent voice of an Irish sergeant—*"Adjust thim shakos! O'Hara! That's a muskit ye're carrying, not a giddy walking stick! Look alive, man!"*

The company commanders moved out before the first line. They marched easily without the one hundred pounds of accouterment each regular labored under. The platoon sergeants marched on the left flank of each company; behind them came the cornets and the line of drummers.

"Hup—hup—hup!" the sergeants growled.

The slope started underfoot and the terrain was rough. The regulars stumbled, caught themselves, and fell back into step. The thick green weeds and meadow grass rose to meet them, obscuring their black gaiters and scraping the tails of their long button-back coats.

Nat glanced down at his left. Everywhere he could see the Americans crouching in tense anticipation under their floppy hats. Along the rail fence and stone wall they were standing in groups of three, one behind the other. Only the front men would fire first; then the second would step up; then the third.

The British crossed a rutted road, and the slope became

a steep agony for overburdened legs. They were approaching a low stone wall that seemed to sling its length around
the full half-circle of the hill. Copp's Battery fell silent, and
the broadsides from the men-of-war died with a running
echo. No sound could be heard from the redoubt on the hill
or the rail fence in the marsh. Nothing moved. An uneasy
silence pervaded the hot, smoky air. A waiting silence.

A breeze from the Mystic River blew across the meadow,
unfurling the folds of the flags and flapped them in the
pulsating air. The bright bayonets stood straight above the
bearskin shakos of the regulars and winked in the sun's
lemon glare like thousands of spearheads fastened on a red
belt. They came on, on . . . .

Drumm-drumm, the drums said to them.

Now they were on the last leg of the march. A hundred

and fifty feet of tall grass separated them from the rail fence, from the stone wall and the flèches. Nat raised his musket.

The drum taps died. All sound had fallen into a deep well of expectancy. The regulars watched the rail fence come slowly toward them, their faces dark and wet, their uniforms turning to sweaty pulp. They blinked their staring eyes vigorously against the dripping moisture that blurred their vision. They opened their mouths and sucked at the thick air. Beyond the rim of the rail fence Bunker Hill stood stark and unreal against the lurid sky.

Grabbit! Nat raged. Why didn't something happen? Those redcoats were so close now he could actually make out the G.R. monogram on the brass plates on the front of their heavy hats.

Suddenly he felt wide open and vulnerable, very vul-

nerable. In fact—except for the grass he was kneeling in—
he was the only American who was in the open. The British
came closer, closer . . . .

A nervous voice rasped beyond the rail fence. "Well, *I*
can see the whites of their eyes. What we waitin' for—a
wink?"

In the flèches, along the rail fence, behind the stone wall,
a bristling row of musket barrels came to the horizontal.
And then one word, a screech of ecstasy——

"FIRE!"

A holocaust blossomed across the meadow. *KA-BAL-
ROOMM!* And the fence vanished under a fat, unrolled
ribbon of white smoke. An invisible scythe mowed through
the red ranks, prostrating platoons and companies as though
they were no more than the long grass through which they
were wading. Flags and muskets fell to the earth like tall
lilies in a mown meadow, and the bayonets stuck in the
ground forming a curious and irregular fence of bobbing
musket butts. Bitterns rose out of the shore reeds in a
flapping panic, going, *gra-awk! gra-awk!*

Nat took a sight on a shouting captain and squeezed, and
the officer's head snapped as though one of his own men
were holding him in leash. The bright gorget at his throat
sprang up and landed in his open mouth, and he fell back
into a sergeant's arms with the silver-plated ornament for a
grin, and the sergeant spilled the captain into the weeds.

Three hundred regulars were down, twisting and squirm-
ing over one another like a mass of red and white worms
bedded in a box of grass. Those that remained on their feet
moved in vague, aimless directions, faces stupid with shock
as they reached for the nothingness of air with empty hands,
their mouths working up and down soundlessly like fish

caught out of water, and one man was trying to explain to his friends that he had a bullet where he had no use for it and how could he go forward or backward or anywhere with a thing like that in his stomach and why for gad's sake didn't they stop and help him, but no one could hear him for the noise.

A captain from the Fifty-second stumbled forward a few paces. He was supporting a wounded corporal. The captain waved the basket-hilt of his sword in the air. He didn't seem to realize that the blade had been shot away. Hat gone, wig gone, his face aglow with maniacal fury, he screamed, "Charge! Charge the bloody swine!" A second volley blew them into a pair of acrobats. They spun off in a crimson somersault.

The bugles blared in a frenzy, the shrieking notes quivering the hot air like heat waves. Suddenly an unseen hand of terror swept through the minds of the regulars, and they turned, bleating fear, and raced back across the marsh for Morton's Point. Officers stood among them, slashing with the flats of their swords, cursing them, imploring them to form up and continue the advance. The regulars went past them as though they didn't exist. The panic was on.

Nat spotted a young ensign crawling through the grass toward the foremost flèche. His eyes were staring from his face in glassy intentness and his slack mouth drooled pink saliva. The scarlet of his tunic was black with blood. A sergeant from the Fifth rose out of the weeds and shouted at him.

"No! Mr. Hawkins, come back!"

Nat saw Shad haul himself out of his trench, calling, "Don't none a you hicks shoot the lad! He can't see what he's doin'."

Ensign Hawkins made it to the trench—the only English soldier who did. He crumpled against the raised earth and slid down to the tall grass, leaving a thin band of blood along the face of the fresh dirt.

"I'm not afraid," he muttered to himself.

"Of course you ain't, boy," Shad said, and he picked up the young ensign gently, as the sergeant from the Fifth started backing away. The smoke had cleared, and he could see the strained faces of the Americans moving behind the flèches, and Shad standing directly in front of him.

"Don't fire," the sergeant said to them. "For gad's sake, don't."

"*Run,* lobsterback!" Shad snapped. The sergeant turned —and he ran.

Nat sat back on his haunches with a shuddering sigh. Shad had been right: war wasn't a tidy officer dying serenely in the arms of his friends with flags waving over his wigged head. War was that young ensign on his hands and knees in the weed.

On the beach the surviving officers and NCO's were trying to regroup the King's demoralized troops. Howe and Pigot and Clinton (who had just arrived alone on the battlefield) were standing in an equipment-littered meadow staring up at the cluttered slope in a strained silence. They seemed nonplussed. Not only had Howe been whipped to a frazzle at the rail fence, but so had Pigot on Breed's Hill.

Clinton's voice rose angrily against the faraway cries of the wounded and the triumphant shouts of the Americans that went up from the crest of Breed's Hill.

"Gad's my life! Gage has a lot to be proud of! He brought on the Lexington fiasco, and now *this* mess! We'll just march up the hill and scare them all away, *he says*. Well, what does he say now?"

"Careful," Pigot advised, "—the men might overhear."

"Let 'em!" Clinton cried. "I don't care who hears me! Gage will have to answer for this. That rabble has no *intention* of running!"

"I can't believe it," Howe murmured wonderingly. "I simply can't believe it happened."

Neither could the Americans, frankly. Nat found them in a wild state of exultation behind the breastwork. They—the untrained, undisciplined, ill-equipped farmers—had stood up to the British regulars. They had whipped the best fighting force in the world.

The Dutch squire who had come all the way from Pennsylvania spotted Nat and raised his fowling piece. "Py tam, poy, mine gun von't carry put thirdy paces, yed dot's how close a Pritisher vas vhen I hid him!"

Prescott was going along the line praising his men, but warning them not to think for a moment that the battle was over. "They'll be back. They're British regulars. Howe won't be stopped by one repulse."

"Sir," Nat reported. "Captain Knowlton says he can hold that fence all day if he receives more powder and shot. Colonel Stark's men accounted for ninety-six redcoats on the beach alone."

"Is Knowlton out of his mind?" Prescott wanted to know. "Where does he think I'll get more powder—out of the sky? Do you know what we're trying to hold our entire line with? Less than eight hundred men. And we average about half a gill of powder per man!"

With a harassed gesture he turned to look across at Bunker Hill. There, and farther on—across the Neck—

were about a thousand idle men milling around, doing absolutely nothing.

"I hope," he said bitterly, "that a monument is someday raised for this battle. I would like it to read: To the cowards who hid on Bunker Hill, while their countrymen fought and died on Breed's."

Nat found a vacant spot along the breastwork and took the position. He reloaded his musket, looking down the trampled slope, across the meadow and to the beach. It was four o'clock, and Howe was aligning his regulars for the second attack.

He had abandoned the idea of flanking Breed's Hill. He sent his light infantry forward to engage Knowlton's attention at the fence, while he and Pigot led everything they had in one slam-bang attack against the redoubt and breastwork.

Nat rested his musket on the breastwork and watched the British come on. They recrossed the meadows, the road, went over the stone wall again. Bearskin shakos littered the grassy slope like round-rumped sleeping racoons; packs, Tower muskets, canteens, cartouche boxes marked the disordered retreat of the first attack. Forty yards below the breastwork sprawled the long, twisted red and white ribbon of the dead and wounded.

The drums rattled insistently now. The officers before the thin red line cursed soft fervent oaths and glanced over their shoulders every few seconds as if to assure themselves that the troops were still behind them.

A rangy backwoodsman in deerskin, with the word *Liberty* printed on his chest in white paint, nudged Nat and drawled: "You think we didn't hurt their officers much, bub? Just looky there at how many of their companies is being led by sergeants'n' corporals."

It was true: the first attack had cost Howe a high toll in officers—their gorgeous uniforms, it seemed, made dandy American targets.

Many of the regulars were marching without their hats, without their wigs. Many wore bandages around their heads.

"You got to hand it to 'em," Nat muttered. "They've got guts."

The backwoodsman switched cheeks with his chaw of tobacco and spat.

"Guts, yeah. But not much sense. They say we're too independent. Well, mebbe so. But I'd druther use my own brainbox in a fight than be like them poor slobs. You take away their officers'n' noncoms and they're lost. They got to be told when to powder their wigs and when to lace their gaiters and when to blow their nose."

Maybe he's right, Nat thought. *Maybe that's what's wrong with Europe: they aren't used to individual thought.* One man had to tell thousands what to do and when to do it and, right or wrong, they did it. But Americans were different. Each man liked to make his own decision, stand on his own feet. Why was that? he wondered. *Perhaps because of our heritage—the heritage of this vast raw savage giant of a land; because right from the beginning we had to go out on our own and establish our camps, forts, towns in a howling wilderness, with no one to back us up, relying only on our own fortitude and ingenuity. And because of that— even though we're late starters—we've got a jump on the rest of the world.*

He looked down at the oncoming regulars again and cocked the wheel lock on his musket. For the first time that day he was eager to fight.

The regulars were approaching the crumpled scarlet ribbon left behind by Pigot's first attempt against the hill, and tension ran through the line as though the soldiers were strung together by wire. The scarlet and white of the moving line reached the scarlet and white of the dead, blended with it, passed on. A deathly silence hovered over the rebel redoubt and breastwork.

We'd better fire, Nat thought. *Heyday, we'd better stop 'em before it's too late.* A hundred and ten feet . . . a hundred feet . . . *Are they going to make it? They're almost here! Good Lord, why don't we*——

"FIRE! FIRE! FIRE!"

A solid bank of snow-white smoke obscured the entire length of the British advance from the redoubt clear down to the stone wall on the beach as eight hundred orange fingers of flame jabbed at the regulars.

Nat felt the kick of the butt in his shoulder and the leap of the barrel in his right hand and tasted, smelled, went blind with the acrid powder smoke. A *whoosh* of hot air seemed to blow through the regulars. The sky was coming down on them, running away from them. They went over backwards, hitting the ground with their heads aimed downhill, the thick blades of grass stabbing around them. It was as though a great wind had struck a window of red autumn leaves, fluttered them in a flurry of color and swept on, leaving them tumbled and still to rot on the green hillside.

A Yankee-nasal voice, insane with emotion, cried:

"Lookit 'em roll! Oh, I tell you boys—*they're through!*"

But they weren't. Those who had lived through the holocaust tried to stand their ground and fight back, as their officers and NCO's ran among the disheveled ranks, pushing, shouting, cursing.

"Form up! Form up! Cawn't you return their fire? Gad's my life! *Don't run without firing a shot!*"

A ragged volley flared from the regulars, but the Americans weren't in a mood for play. Those long brittle-bright bayonets were too close for comfort. Sheet after sheet of orange roaring bucking fire blasted out of the redoubt and breastwork. Nat, coughing, drenched with sweat, half-blinded, loaded, set up a smear of crimson in the front sight, fired, stepped back, reaching for powderhorn, musket ball . . .

All at once the backwoodsman dropped his gun, grabbed at his neck with both hands, spinning half around, paused, staring wildly at Nat with iron-hard eyes, tried to say something but only made a gurgle of it, kept on turning, then took two-three steps away and sank to one knee. There was nothing Nat could do about it. Rules of combat. He loaded, fired, stepped back, loaded . . .

The second retreat was already underway. This time it was actually ordered by Pigot—who simply could not believe the brickwall of fire he had butted his head into.

The British poured back down the hill helter-skelter, every man for himself, running frantically away from that deadly wall of drifting smoke. Nat heard a gargled voice call— "Are ye with me, O'Hara? O'Hara! Tis yersilf I'm——"

But the rest of it was drowned under the victory shout of the Americans which rose tumultuously on the troubled air. Nat lowered his hot musket and looked over the breastwork. He saw a mottle-faced major standing knee-high in the grass, striking at the fleeing regulars with his sword. His open mouth was a great bawling pit, and his words fell strangely on Nat's ears.

"Demn your eyes! Will no man make a stand with me? Am I cursed to command craven cowards? Twenty pounds to the man that will go back up the hill with me! Twenty pounds *from my own pocket!*"

Wonder of wonders! Until this day an order given by a Royal officer or NCO was never questioned, never delayed, but acted upon instantly. And now on this strange scarred slope of battled ground a major stood among his men like a reed in the wind and begged, berated, bribed them to form a line!

"What news!" Nat heard Shad's familiar cry ring across the slope, and, looking out, he spotted his friend trotting along the upper face of the hill, waving a hatchet he'd picked up somewhere. About ten of his farmboy recruits were following him. Shad stopped all at once and faced the red-faced major. They were about fifty feet apart.

To the surprise of the Americans on the hill, Shad highballed a proper salute to the furiously distracted British major, calling:

"Major Totten! You best git to heck'n' gone out a here! These boys is redcoat-hungry today!"

The major caught his breath and looked stark-eyed at Shad, then blinked, then shoved out his head and looked again.

"I remember you! You saved my life at Braddock's Field when I was an ensign! If you think you're saving it again today you're mistaken! I don't want any favors from any rebels!"

"Major," Shad bawled, "I know you don't. But you can't take that hill by yourself, you know! Now git out a here while you're still in one piece—sir!"

Major Totten turned and shook his fist at the breastwork, then—defiantly—spun on his heel and started down the hill, walking.

Shad yelled at the Americans: "I'll bust the gravy out a any hick that fires on that limey! By grab, he's *a man* he is!" Then he came lumbering over the breastwork, shouting: "Where's Nat Towne! By Oswald's outhouse, I got him into this shindig and if I hear that anything's happened to him, I'm gonna take somebody by the——"

Nat, grinning, his eyes honestly brimming with tears he couldn't help or understand or cared a hoot about, caught his big friend's arm.

"Shad—you're the best man I've ever known! I'm almighty thankful you saved that man's life."

Shad blinked at him. "Who—the major? Listen, Natty, when I saved him twenty years ago next month, he was shot in the hip and he was seventeen years old and so scared he'd chawed all the nails off his right fingers and was startin' on his left. Since then he's grown up to be a man, he has, and I don't see no sense in wastin' a real man—no matter *what* side he's on!"

We're not bad men, Nat thought again. *We're merely men doing a dirty job that has to be done.*

The regulars didn't pause until they reached the beach, and a few went so far as to climb into the barges. But by now 400 fresh men had been sent over from Boston, and Howe (whose mind had not been trained for retreat) gave the order to advance for the third time, in spite of the entreaties of some of his officers who stated that it would be plain murder to send his men up the hill again.

Howe was a man obsessed. He was going to take that hill and that's all there was to it. He ordered that all packs should be removed plus any other equipment that might encumber his troops.

"This is to be a bayonet charge," he instructed his junior officers.

He also set his fieldpieces in the meadows and concentrated a raking fire on the breastwork. In a moment the beach was divided by a canvass wall as the regulars laid aside their eighty-pound packs. Then the battery on Copp's Hill awoke with an angry explosion, and shells began to wing toward the redoubt.

Before the advancing regulars had reached the low lying meadows, the smoke of Charlestown had rolled up to the crest of Breed's Hill in the shape of a great black cloud mass. Nat and Shad hunkered down side by side as the British shells began a vindictive pounding against the works. Their position was untenable. Major Moore, in command of the breastwork, ordered everyone inside the redoubt.

The first thing Nat heard as he entered the three-sided fort was the cry for powder. In their desperation the Americans were breaking open the cannon cartridges Gridley and Callender had left behind. But it was a precious small amount each man received. Shad joggled the hatchet in his belt and grinned at Nat.

"I've used a tomahawk agin bay'nets afore this. Surprising how much damage you can do with one—if you know the trick."

Again Howe watched the crest of the hill loom before him, slightly obscured now by the coils of heavy smoke, and, possibly, he made his only prayer for the day: *If I fall this time—please—let the rest of the lads go on. Let there be an end to the retreats.* This much must be said for Howe: he led all three attacks himself. True, he was the sad product of the European battlefields, but he would not send his men into any position, no matter how deadly, without leading the way himself. *Noblesse oblige*, it was called.

They approached the first line of British dead, but they didn't glance down. Their eyes were fixed on the redoubt. The goal. They stepped over their own silent comrades and moved up to the second line of carnage. A captain, left behind at the end of the second charge, looked up at them from the grass, his eyes curiously white in a mask of dripping red.

"All the way this time, chaps," he whispered to them. "Remember you are British regulars."

British regulars . . . so close now Nat could see the sweat on their faces. Hurriedly he checked his equipment. He had a charge for each pistol and just about enough powder and ball for his musket for three shots. What would happen after that he had no idea.

The regulars stepped through the second line of dead and wounded and faced the ditch and the soft new earth of the redoubt. The muskets behind the parapet ran up like pickets on a fence, then swept down to the horizontal. Nat sucked his breath, took a sight, and——

"FIRE! FIRE! FIRE!"

Once more under the recoil of the muskets the parapet blossomed a sheet of white and orange, and the whithering blast swept the thin red line apart. It *plam-plam-plammed* from the redoubt, the breastwork, the flèches, and the rail fence, and it was downright murderous. But this time there was no panic. The British meant to take that hill.

Howe deployed his men and had them advance in open order, twelve feet apart in the front, but very close after each other in deep files. Nat noticed that as fast as the front man was shot down the next in line stepped into his place. The fire power behind the American blow had waned. The charm seemed to have ended. The scarlet line trembled, sagged, filled in again, came on.

But not fast. The Americans were dropping them as quickly as the second, third, fourth man could step up to his fallen comrade's place. And then the British made a mistake that cost them even more dearly. Howe's order had been for a bayonet charge only; but the regulars couldn't seem to get close enough to bring their bayonets into play. So they started to hang back and return the Americans' fire.

The officers and NCO's were simply beside themselves trying to keep the companies in formation. "Push on! Push on! Don't stop now!"

"Hold 'em! Hold 'em back!" Prescott's voice roared through the din and smoke. "*Now! Now!* Pour it to 'em!"

The Americans rose on their parapet and cut loose with everything they had, and the *pak! pak! pak!* of the kicking muskets was something to marvel over, while the Royal officers kept right on shoving, cursing, screaming in the regulars' ears.

"*Over! Go over!* Form up! Bayonets! *Bayonets!*"

Nat's musket had had it; no more powder or ball. He looked around at the powder-blackened faces of the citizen-soldiers. Many of them were already in the same fix. Some were firing nails or small lead buttons or any bit of metal they could find on the ground. Then men began picking up stones, and they fought with them like street boys in a rock fight.

The regulars stumbled and lurched into a semblance of a line, boots slipping over the thrashing bodies of the wounded, over the still bodies of the dead. They came falling and sliding down into the ditch at the foot of the redoubt, and it was one of the few instances where troops (let alone farmers) continued to defend a redoubt after the enemy had infiltrated the ditch. But the Americans in the little fort were as determined to hang onto that hill as the British were to take it, and they fought like men possessed —with shot and clubbed muskets and rocks and bare fists, and the faces were the same wild angry cursing iron-eyed faces that had waded into the Menotomy road to fight the regulars hand to hand.

A bayonet flashed over the rim of the redoubt, and then another and another, and Nat ducked fast as British fire flew overhead and saw five men of Gershom Smith's company go down right in front of him, and saw too a man called Brown grab for the falling Smith, change his mind, let him go, fire his musket, then reach for Smith's and fire it, and then leap for the first regular coming over the parapet and snatch the soldier's musket right out of his hands, turn it on him, and blow the redcoat back into the ditch below.

Nat on one knee brought up his right pistol and bowled over a tall corporal who had just scrambled to the top of the works. Crouching there at the right salient angle of the redoubt, he looked at the pistol in his left hand. Last shot.

The bright bayonets rose, came down, cutting a long line of winking light in the colorless air. And then they were climbing up, and everywhere the command *"OVER! OVER!"* sounded. All around Nat the unequal hand-to-hand melee surged back and forth and, because his countrymen were fighting back bayonets with nothing but rocks and fists and guts, he suddenly experienced a deeply searing sense of hate and tasted the bittersweet taste of revenge in his dry mouth.

Just beyond the wall an officer of Pigot's wave was bawling his men on, shouting: "On! On! They've abandoned the fort!"

"We're not *all* gone!" Nat yelled with a consuming fury.

And he rose, cocking the pistol, and deliberately leveled it over the parapet, catching a full view of the officer who was just then approaching the ditch with his sword waving over his head, and he fired point-blank.

He ducked again as the marines cut loose at him with their muskets, the balls going *fut-fut-fut* in the dirt along the rim of the wall.

"They've killed Major Pitcairn!" a dozen voices rose in a wail. "We've lost a father!"

Bleakly, Nat looked at the empty pistol in his hand. *Almost as if for an inexorable purpose . . .*

The regulars were coming at the wall as though they meant to tear it apart with fingers, feet, and teeth. They were coming over by the hundreds, and their bayonets were clearing a flashing path through the fist-flailing, musket-clubbing, hate-cursing Yankees. They were blood-mad with the held-back fury that had been building within them that long grim afternoon. They had two hours of torture on the littered slope of Breed's Hill to make up for, and they were doing it in the only way a combat soldier fighting in close quarters can do it.

Compassion and quarter were archaically romantic words for other battles fought in other places in another style, long long ago.

Nat simply couldn't see where he was going. The dust and smoke was as thick and opaque as a solid wall. But it was this very block of blinding smoke that kept the redoubt from becoming a deathtrap for the Yankees; the British couldn't find, couldn't see the enemy. Prescott, his dueling sword flashing in the spectral gloom, knew it was over.

"Fall back! Fall back!" his disembodied voice rose again and again.

A militia captain bumped against Nat, swung up his musket and potted a leaping British officer, then made a blind rush for the redoubt's only exit, holding his gun broadwise before his face to keep from being clubbed. Nat started feeling his way along the right wall, heading for the rear, shoving aside and pushing through a quagmire-like nightmare of shadowy half figures.

He saw Prescott dimly. The colonel refused to run. He strode toward the exit with his head hunched, warding off blows with his sword.

All at once the smoke thinned and Nat stumbled into the clear. Someone slammed against him, and he spun about with his heart high in his throat and saw Dr. Warren looking at him with a glassy-eyed look that was no look at all. Warren went down dead at Nat's feet.

"Doctor," Nat said. "*Ah, Doctor,* I . . . "

"Leave that, Towne!" Prescott's voice cut at him. "Worry about the wounded!"

Nat turned away from the body of the man whom Lord Rawdon (Rawdon himself, at that very moment, was in the bottom of the ditch in front of the redoubt, so pinned down he couldn't get over the wall) had called "the greatest incendiary in all America." He turned bewilderedly, almost aimlessly, and spotted the portly, red-faced Dutch squire from Pennsylvania down on the trampled ground on his left side, clutching a shattered right kneecap. The Dutchman looked up at him with round blue baby eyes, but said nothing.

"All right," Nat said, crouching down. "All right. I'm here."

The Dutchman shook his head. "You candt do hid, poy. I'm too heavy for you."

"Shut up! Just shut up!" Nat raged, trying, straining, coming to tears as he attempted to jack the fat man up from the ground.

A perfect wheel of fighting fury came boiling out of the smoky exit of the redoubt: Shad Holly, with one regular caught by the neck under the crook of his right arm—Shad landing sledgehammer blows off the top of the thrashing, yelling man's hatless head—and another regular dragging along at his left hip with his arms about Shad's waist, and Shad giving him left elbow jabs in the face in between the hammer blows he was pounding home on the other soldier's head.

Lurching and staggering sweatily along with a most remarkable string of curse words, Shad finally raised his right arm and let that regular take a pancake dive into the dirt (and he, the regular, stayed that way too—flat), then he angled his huge body about and got a clutch on the scruff of the other regular's neck with his left and raised the man clear off the ground and swung him inward, at the same time bringing his right fist up to make contact with the regular's face, and *Bap!* that was another Englishman who was going to need a set of whalebone teeth. Dusting his hands, Shad started to look around for more action.

"Lookout behind you, Shad!" Nat yelled.

Shad tossed a glance over his shoulder and saw a regular emerging from the undulating smoke with a leveled bayonet. Shad started running away. But not far. Only far enough to draw the hatchet he'd picked up from somewhere from his belt. Then he stopped and turned back as the redcoat charged with a triumphant yell.

"*COO-WEEGH-HHH!*" Shad shrieked and he skimmed that hatchet through the air like a tomahawk, and it hit so hard and true that the regular made a one-point landing on the back of his head.

"Shad! Help me with this Dutchman!"

Shad came trotting over with an angry look on his big dripping face.

"My goodness, Natty, ain't you got no sense a-tall? You want a bust a gut or something in you? Here, give him to me."

Shad got the man under the armpits and raised him, facing him, then ducked his burly head and shoulder into the Dutchman's midriff, jackknifing him, and straightened up, holding him in the fireman's carry.

"Cover us with them pistols of yours," he told Nat.

"They're both empty."

"Well, *pretend* they ain't! You don't have to let the lobsterbacks know it, do you?" They started down the back slope of Breed's Hill.

All around and ahead and behind them the Americans were retreating. Because it was over. And the Americans would say that they had won, and the British would say No, *they* had won, and History—indecisively compromising—would call it a draw. But all that really mattered at the moment was—it was over.

16

THIS GREAT LAND FORTRESS

There was no rout. It was not a panic. The American withdrawal was so orderly in fact that they were able to carry off all their wounded except 31 mortally injured—who were the only prisoners the British took.

And they begrudged every yard of ground they had to give. The men from the rail fence and stone wall, plus the troops from Bunker Hill (who finally decided to get into the fight), gathered along the walls in the meadows and covered the retreat of the Yankees from Breed's Hill. They maintained a running fight from wall to fence to tree which kept the British advance in a tight check.

Nat, striding a little behind Shad and his burden, his useless pistols clenched in his sweaty hands, spotted old Seth Pomeroy walking backwards over the meadow, still belligerently facing the British. His ancient musket was at the ready, but its stock had been shattered by a ball. It was the most diehard method of retreat Nat ever hoped to see.

"Shad," Nat called. "Did you *see* them up on that hill? Did you see 'em fighting with rocks? *Rocks! Against bayonets!*"

"Shut up, Nat! Don't let it get you. You're gonna see more'n that afore this here war's over. By grab, once these Yankees get to fightin' they just won't give up!"

They passed a line of Bunker Hill men firing furiously from behind a stone wall. Old Put, hatless and shirtsleeves rolled up, was holding out his hands to Prescott.

"There was nothing I could *do,* Will! I couldn't get you support. I couldn't *drive* the dogs!"

"If you couldn't drive them up, you might have *led* them up!" Prescott snapped. He was in a foul temper. He had almost won a great battle, and he knew it. Just one more round of ammo for his men and he was certain he would have stopped the British for good at the ditch.

But it wasn't really fair to blame Putnam; anyone could see at a glance that the tough old veteran had done his best. How many times he'd rode back and forth over the Neck under cannon fire to try to find support for Prescott no one would ever know. He was near tears.

And there was still more to come to cry over. The Neck had to be crossed by the fagged Yankee army—and the Neck was under a savage raking fire from the *Glasgow.* The retreating army found itself bunched up in a funnel-like deathtrap—the shell and grapeshot slamming and whining across the road, gouging up deep furrows in the sand, themselves stumbling and cursing over their own dropping wounded, and going back to pick them up, and men hit so square you'd need a shovel to pick them up, and the gosh-awful scattered discarded equipment everywhere underfoot, and then that fool Dutchman began pounding on Shad's back.

"*Pud me down!* You candt make hid mit me!" And Shad yelling back:

"Shut your fat face, Dutchy! I could run with three like you! Go on, Nat! Leg it across. We'll be all right!"

"No." Nat shook his head. "No." Then he cringed as something as big and heavy as an iron stove came howling overhead. But he wouldn't run. He stayed behind Shad, still covering for him with those worthless pistols.

The battered, dirty, shirtsleeved army trundled across the chaotic Neck and straggled wearily down the dust-churned road to Cambridge. Shad and Nat found a wagon loading wounded and they placed the groaning Dutchman into the straw-littered bed. He nodded at them grimly.

"Thanks, poys. Mine vife, she vill——"

Shad patted the man's good leg and grinned. "Sure, Dutchy. Don't mention it. Us Pennsylvanians showed 'em, didn't we?"

Putnam was leading the bushed troops to Winter and Prospect hills, there to go to work digging an entrenchment 100 feet square. Where these men—who had been on their feet for 36 hours, marching, taking cannon fire, facing frontal assaults, bayonet attacks, and hand-to-hand combat, without food or water or rest—found the energy to dig a new fort is a wonderful mystery. But they did it.

Colonel Stark was holding the rearguard at the Neck, and Nat and Shad parked themselves groaningly under an elm, thinking they might come in use somehow.

"Got any powder left?" Nat asked. Shad shook his head. "Nope. And no gun to use it in did I have any."

Nat sighed and put his pistols away. He kept hearing the voices of those marines wailing, *We've lost a father! We've lost a father!* Yes—the original owner of those pistols had been quite a man.

Out in the road he saw the towering Major McClary

talking to Stark. The colonel was pointing back at Bunker Hill, where General Clinton's detachment could be seen moving over the crest. Nat heard McClary's voice rise in a good-natured boom.

"Well, you'd just as soon be certain they *don't* plan on crossing over and coming after us, wouldn't you? And it wouldn't be safe to take a squad back over the Neck. Make too tempting a target. It's a one-man job." Then Stark said something that Nat didn't catch, and McClary laughed. "Stop fretting, John. I eat lobsterbacks for supper!"

A moment later McClary started back across the Neck alone, to make a final reconnaissance on the British. It was a shade after five-thirty and dusk was spreading over the distant battlefield. Breathlessly the Yankees on the mainland watched the tall figure of the major make his way boldly almost to the foot of Bunker Hill. Evidently he was satisfied that the British had had enough for the day, for Nat saw him raise his hat and wave it toward the mainland.

Then McClary started back across the Neck in the winy twilight.

The *Glasgow* swung lazily on her cable and touched off a parting salute from one of her larboard cannons. It was the last shot of that long shot-riddled day.

One moment McClary's great form was silhouetted in stride against the afterglow on the Neck. . . . The next moment he was gone, completely.

A ringing cry of rage and despair sprang from the throats of the watching Yankees. And Shad shoved up to his feet, bawling:

"You didn't have to do that! You lousy lobsterbacked sons of——"

But Colonel Stark turned to him with a heavy look and

shook his head. "Be glad, Sergeant," he said. "It would have been a sin to have killed that gigantic hero with any weapon *less* than a cannon."

Shad blinked blankly at the colonel, then slowly drew the back of his wrist across his mouth. He sat down again beside Nat, staring out at the empty Neck.

"You know something, Natty? When Stark went to build the stone wall, he left McClary and his company behind the rail fence to help Knowlton. It was McClary's presence that gave them Connecticutters their courage. I could see him from my trench, going up and down the line laughin' and jokin' with the fellas, giving 'em encouragement. And you know something else? He *was* the biggest man in the American army."

It was two days after the battle of Breed's Hill (which, due to the error of British army cartographers, became known as the Battle of Bunker's Hill) when Nat and Shad were finally able to locate General Putnam in his Harvard quarters.

Old Put looked like something the cat had dragged in and then decided it wasn't worth keeping. He was in the same clothes that he had donned on the morning of the sixteenth; in fact he hadn't been out of them once. Nor had he been doing much sleeping.

Sitting there at the head of the table like a squat toad in shirtsleeves, he looked at Nat and Shad with red-rimmed eyes, then motioned toward a paper spread before him.

"My aide with the mathematical mind just gave me the latest butcher's bill," he said. "Out of twenty-four hundred British troops and officers, we hit one thousand fifty-four." He paused and looked up from the paper with a wistful smile. "That's better than double what Howe said he'd give to take Dr. Warren."

"Good!" Shad said grimly. "At least they paid for that."

Putnam looked at the paper again. "We had four hundred forty-one casualties out of a possible fifteen hundred combatants. This figure includes all those gutless wonders I couldn't move off of Bunker Hill. One hundred forty dead, two hundred seventy wounded, and thirty-one captured." He shoved the paper aside and sagged back in his chair with a heavy sigh. Shad leaned over the table belligerently.

"But we *won*, didn't we, General? Gol-dummit, we had 'em licked right up to the last minute! If we'd've had the powder . . . " His voice turned insistent. "General—we won her, didn't we?"

Old Put stared at the table for a long bemused moment. Then he said, "Technically, no. But virtually, yes. It was an American victory. We whipped 'em blind two times out of three; and we retreated only when our ammo was exhausted. And, boys, there will *never* be another retreat like that one —not where farmers stand up with nothing but rocks against redcoat bayonets!"

Shad nodded and straightened up.

"That's what I been tellin' ever'body that warn't there." He glanced at the bruised knuckles on his right fist. "Sometimes I've had to tell some of 'em behind the barracks— when there ain't no officers around."

Putnam grinned and turned to Nat. "What was this Indian business you've been wanting to see me about, Towne?"

Nat told him the story of the Abenaki message, then he drew the roll of birchbark over his head and handed it to the general. Old Put went for Abenaki the way a bee goes for a buttercup. He unrolled the strip of bark and started mumbling a translation to himself.

"It's from that renegade Paul Higgins . . . he speaks for the sachems of the Androscoggin and Kennebec Abenakis. In reply to the Seneca tribes as to whether the Abenakis will take up the hatchet for the English or the Americans, he says that the Abenakis have no intention of fighting the Americans. He goes on to say that the Abenakis, under his jurisdiction, desire to *fight* the British! More—he says that it is their wish to make an assault with the Americans against Quebec!"

Nat let out his breath. So—in truth, the Abenaki message had read the exact opposite from what Jessie Greene had told the Committee two months before. The Abenakis wanted to be American allies!

"This will be mighty good news to Washington," Old Put said.

"Washington?" Shad echoed.

Putnam nodded. "George Washington is going to take command of the provincial army," he told them. "He's due to arrive here in two weeks."

"Washington," Shad said, and he turned to Nat with a look that was indescribable.

Nat himself felt an uplift of relief. For the first time he felt that the provincials and their colonies were in good hands. There was something godlike about Washington, to the men who knew him, to those who had fought beside him in the French and Indian War, and to those who knew him only by name. Washington . . . it was a name with meaning.

"Holly," Putnam said, "there's a good possibility that the Seneca will throw in with us once they learn the nature of this Abenaki message. Not all of them, perhaps—but if only a few tribes decide to raise the hatchet against the English, we'll have allies well worth cultivating. With that purpose in mind, someone who knows the Seneca and their language should go along the New York and Pennsylvania frontier and show this message to the tribes."

Shad nodded. "I suppose you got me in mind, General?"

Old Put grinned at him. "I don't know a better man for the job."

"General," Nat said, "will you include me in that order? Aside from the fact that I promised that dying messenger I'd keep the birchbark personally—Shad and I have a sort of partnership interest in this war."

Putnam stared at him reflectively with his tired eyes, then nodded.

"I don't see how I can refuse, Towne. This part of the show belongs to you." He glanced at Shad and spoke in the tongue-tying dialect of the Seneca. *"Ne gwa, gi'on, hadi'nonge ne hen'non'gwe"* (The beginning belongs to youth).

"Da. Onen. Na'e!" (Yes, now it is so!) Shad replied.

Nat removed the major's pistols from his belt for the last time and placed them on the table before Putnam.

"I won't be using these again, General," he said quietly. "Major Pitcairn is dead. He was a good man."

Old Put stared at the brace of pistols with tired, sad eyes.

"They were all good men, boy," he said. "Those who fought on top of the hill—as well as those who fought to gain the top."

With the first cold strips of horizon dawn, Nat and Shad mounted the horses Putnam had commandeered for them.

Nat glanced at his partner, and Shad winked at him. Then Nat looked off across the hills, across the Mystic River, at the strange dark land that spread before him. Thousands of miles of it, he'd been told; high with great mountains, thick with vast forests, barren with arid deserts, rutted with deep canyons, split by massive lakes and endless rivers.

This was the land of the people called the Rabble. And the British had just captured one small hill at the very fringe of this great land fortress—at the cost of over a thousand men.

Suddenly—at the thought of the absurdity of it—Nat started to laugh.

"What news?" Shad asked.

"Onward," Nat said. Alone together they rode into their strange new world, seeking. The gates of Gibby's prison stood wide open before them.

www.ingramcontent.com/pod-product-compliance
Lightning Source LLC
Chambersburg PA
CBHW031401250626
47155CB00004B/1360